ABOUT THE AUTHOR

Laura grew up in a small fishing village in Northumberland and is married with three children. She currently lives with her husband and three boys in Queensland, Australia.

Laura is a qualified counsellor and she has worked in a domestic violence service for the past five years. Seeing the effects of domestic violence, and learning about the complexities of it, spurred her to write her first novel.

Laura enjoys writing and finds it helps her unwind. She decided at a young age that she would love to be an author but never felt as if the time was right. Until now! She looks forward to learning and growing as an author.

DEDICATION

This book is dedicated to all survivors of
domestic violence.

Laura Adams

WITH THIS RING...

AUSTIN MACAULEY PUBLISHERS™

LONDON • CAMBRIDGE • NEW YORK • SHARJAH

A CIP catalogue record for this title is available from the British Library.

ISBN 978-1-78693-154-2 (Paperback)
ISBN 978-1-78693-155-9 (Hardback)
ISBN 978-1-78693-156-6 (E-Book)
www.austinmacauley.com

First Published (2017)
Austin Macauley Publishers Ltd.™
25 Canada Square
Canary Wharf
London
E14 5LQ

ACKNOWLEDGMENTS

I would like to thank my husband, my rock, for supporting me throughout this process, and for never doubting that I would achieve what I set out to do. I love you more than you will ever know.

To my children who made my life complete and who give me so much joy, I love you.

Much love to my sister, who had faith in me and spurred me on when I doubted myself. To my friends that read the manuscript and gave me feedback, I am blessed to have you in my life!

To Andi Wright, who inspired me with her amazing art by painting a picture of a lady that encompassed everything that my main character was about, thank you!

The inspiration for the cover painting was taken from Adriano Trapani, an Italian living in Phuket as a successful photographer. Adriano has an immense catalogue of work behind him and continues to be a inspiration to this day. A link to his website: http://phuketpaparazzi.com/

To Austin Macauley thank you to you and your team, for making this possible.

CHAPTER 1

I threw myself over the side of the boat and gasped as the cool water pushed the air out of my lungs with force. I welcomed the deep blue water rushing over my head, soothing my aching body. I felt weightless and hung around in the water with my eyes closed, savouring the freedom that I felt. If only I could stay here I thought, as I turned and swam with firm strokes towards the darker, deeper blue of the ocean.

I had often imagined myself as a mermaid when I was a child and had wondered if I stayed under water long enough, if I would develop the ability to breathe like a fish; lungs soaked with seawater, miraculously breathing oxygen into my body. I'd pictured myself with a strong emerald green tail that would shimmer and change colour as I moved around the ever-changing ocean. I had visualized myself darting in and out of rocks with luxurious hair flowing behind me, and the sound of other mermaids giggling in the shadows. How I wished that I could transform that thought into reality and swim away my days in oblivion, free and happy, and more importantly, removed from the reality of my frenetic life.

I watched the sand swirling and dancing below me, pushed around by conflicting currents of water, urging each grain to go this way, then that way.

A hermit crab with an overly large shell scurried behind a rock with an urgency that was quite amusing. Chunky coral swayed in the ever changing current, and grabbed out at microscopic algae, while small colourful fish darted in clusters looking like they needed to get somewhere in a hurry, occasionally disappearing in the dark and light colours of the ebbing tide, as sand swirled in puffy clouds each time there was a burst of activity.

A prod on my shoulder brought me back to the present and I turned quickly to see a wide-eyed guide beckoning me frantically back towards the boat. It must be time to leave.

I swam back towards the boat and watched as legs swished crazily back and forth underneath the water, while bodies bobbed up and down. It made me think of the scene from *Titanic*. The one where everyone was in the water splashing for their lives.

However, this particular situation could not have been further removed from that event. I looked at all of the people treading water while they took a breather, chatting excitedly and pointing to the array of activity going on beneath them.

I was on a reef trip in Cairns, but I felt as if I was on board the *Titanic*, slowly sinking and fighting for my life.

I surfaced from the safety net of the ocean and removed the snorkel as I gulped in salty sea air. I tried to steady my rapidly beating heart by swallowing more air into my lungs, and would have laughed at the irony of me looking like a fish out of water, had I not felt so distressed.

Have you ever had that terrifying experience when you inhale but feel as if no air is entering your lungs? In an attempt to calm yourself, you gulp harder to try to and fill the ever growing void. You become focused on air, and the desperate need for it fills you with a feeling of terror. A feeling that causes rising panic to grow like a monster in your chest.

There have been times lately when my body has felt strangely broken. When my head is awash with a terrifying dizziness and my stomach churns like a rough stormy sea. It has filled me with dread and a familiarity that I thought was long gone.

I now found myself with a mind and body that felt as if they had gone two separate ways. I no longer felt in control of my thoughts and would catch myself drifting off for hours into a strange dreamlike state, which would bizarrely pass by like minutes. I would enter a room with a purpose and then find myself staring out of the window half an hour later, unaware of why I had gone in the room in the first place. I put things down and then could not remember doing so, and my razor-sharp mind became confused and unable to retain information. And for the second time in my life, I had walked away. Only this time it would not be so easy to reinvent myself and start again. That day in my office had changed the course of my life faster than I would ever have thought possible, and all of my affirmations and self-beliefs vanished as quickly as a puff of smoke. I had gone home, quickly packed a suitcase and jumped in my car, heading to an unknown destination.

****

I drove out of the buzzing city of Brisbane at two pm on a Tuesday afternoon and headed north. I stopped at Rockhampton and stayed in a motel overnight after a seven-hour drive. I gave little thought to my surroundings, which is so unlike me. I relished the finer things in life and I had worked damn hard to allow myself the luxury of enjoying them. My usual stay over would have been at the Hilton, however, that was before my world came crashing down around me. Suddenly I no longer cared what the surroundings looked like.

After exploring the room, which took me all of one minute, I lay on top of the bedspread, which was splattered with yellow faded flowers and almost threadbare. The walls were off white with scuffmarks and a tacky picture of flowers hung off centre on the back wall. There was a toilet with a pull-to door that refused to close properly, and a showerhead that had seen better days. I was aware of a damp smell that lingered in the room. It reminded me of something from my past and I squeezed my eyes shut forcibly, trying to block out the memories that had started invading my brain like shards of glass. Painful and shockingly vivid; they had started off as splinters with a burst of light and a very vague memory attached, and they had grown in size and frequency. The memories were now the size of an iceberg, with chunks of my past invading my brain. To say it was frightening was an understatement. I have worked very hard to create my new life and forget the past, and now I felt it slowly coming undone, and I did not have the faintest idea how to stop it.

I drifted in and out of sleep, each time feeling disoriented when I woke, but too hazy with mental exhaustion and unable to rouse myself enough to gather my thoughts. I would flop back down and wait desperately to fall into oblivion while hovering in a strangely unrealistic world that I was unfamiliar with.

On waking early in the morning, I grabbed a breakfast muffin and an extra strong coffee and hit the road as soon as I could, determined to put as much distance between myself, and Brisbane as possible.

As I drove northwards I had the sensation of being removed from reality. I would have episodes where my heart would beat wildly, as if I had run a marathon, and my head would spin, giving me the feeling that my whole body was lurching to one side. I felt as if a cage full of birds had been released into my chest, fluttering wildly and sending crazy sensations rippling through my upper half. Twice I had to pull over, and on the second occasion I burst into tears.

The fact that I was crying made me cry even harder and I felt I was losing my grip on reality, as tears forged rivers down my face.

Despite my emotional state, I decided to drive on until I arrived at the next township and then book into a motel. I wanted to remain anonymous and the thought of bumping into a work associate made my stomach tense.

I booked into the first motel I came across in Mackay, which seemed to be a typical tropical town with palm trees swaying in the breeze, and a laid-back attitude to match the setting. The drive had taken six hours so I decided to head to the beach. The busier I was the less time I had to think.

I parked the car and trod over dry snapping twigs, and ground that was stained purple with berries from tamarind trees. I walked onto the beach and was relieved to see that I was by myself. Hardly surprising as it was just after mid-day and the red-hot sun was beating down.

What's that saying? 'Only a mad dog and an Englishman will go out in the hottest part of the day?'

The word Englishman stuck in my brain allowing the past to crash into my present. Creeping and seeping into my thoughts at any opportunity, threatening to shatter my world and everything I had built around it. A fleeting picture of England barged its way to the front of my mind and made my heart skip a beat in the process.

I removed my sandals and took a breath in as the hot dry sand scorched the bottom of my feet. I made quick hopping steps to the cooler damp sand that had recently been soaked by the frothy sea and walked until the point of exhaustion.

I sat down and started grabbing handfuls of warm, dry sand, allowing it to filter through my fingers and form tiny hills that moved as the wind changed. There is something terribly therapeutic about sand, and I fell into that time trap again, unaware of how long I had been sitting as my mind dived between past and present, each time rapidly trying to close the door on the memories of the years gone by.

I stood once I felt my shoulders start to stiffen with the sun and on leaving the beach I headed to a convenience store just over the road, and bought myself a pre-packed sandwich, some fruit, several bottles of water and a pack of painkillers to block out my fierce, beating headache. My next stop was a drive through bottle shop where I bought a six-pack of beer and one bottle of good quality red wine.

I sat on the bed in the dingy room with the television on as a noisy distraction in the background. I opened a bottle of cold beer and drank it until the fizz almost burst out of my nose. I let out a long belch, which was quickly followed by a feeling of shame, and the terrified young girl inside of me that was trying hard to rebel, was quickly silenced.

Although I had no appetite, I forced myself to eat half a cheese and ham sandwich as I sat contemplating whether to turn on my mobile phone. I decided to drink the rest of the beer before thinking about it again and instead focused my attention on a game show that was extremely irritating, but a welcome distraction from the other thoughts flitting through my muddled head.

Six beers later and one glass of strong red wine and I plucked up the courage to switch on the phone. I was still not prepared for the flood of emotions that surged through my body as my phone almost crashed with the sudden flurry of activity. Fifty-two missed calls and dozens of messages. Most from Gregg, my long-term boyfriend who I kept at arm's length, and several from my boss and work colleagues.

I read the first text message: *Charlotte PLEASE call me. I am so worried about you. Where are you? And what the hell has happened for you to take off? Love Gregg.*

The next message read: *Charlotte please answer your phone. I am so worried. I have called Gregg (sorry if I wasn't supposed to but I didn't know what else to do). Tess x*

Tess was my second in command. A pretty, petite girl of twenty-eight who had been married for two years. I was met with disapproval from the board when I promoted her, but my business radar had been spot on and she had turned out to be an absolute gem.

I attempted to listen to the rest of the stored messages but stopped after message four, I simply could not face it. I started sobbing again; huge racking sobs that left me feeling as helpless as a newborn baby. I realized that I did not have a friend to call that would understand my current situation, only work colleagues. I had decided many years ago that it was too risky to have a confidante in my personal life here in Australia.

No, I had decided that it was definitely better to channel energy into a career and only socialize with staff occasionally, and so professionalism won out over companionship.

I am good to my workforce and treat them respectfully provided that when they walk into the office at eight am, they are there to work. No bullshit, that's what I'd tell them, and the ones who had got away with slacking off for too long soon found alternative work elsewhere and I was left with a good team of reliable workers and the scope to bring in some fresh blood. I never used to be so upfront and tough, but life changes you and now I was no longer afraid to say what I thought. I had finally found my voice after years of never being heard.

I had started off as an office worker and then progressed to team leader. From there I was offered head of HR and finally Chief Executive Officer of the Brisbane branch for BRB. I fully absorbed whatever job I was doing and read articles on rival companies during my evenings. Lunch was usually spent sourcing new clients and looking for weaknesses in competing firms. I loved finding a niche that was unfilled and became obsessed at varying stages until I had achieved what I wanted to achieve. I was rewarded highly and the company spared no expense, which I thought extravagant but nonetheless enjoyable. I sipped champagne at luncheons and received triple figure bonus cheques on a frequent basis - and although I was head hunted regularly by bigger organizations that were looking for someone with dedication and no commitments, I always turned them down because I was content where I was, or at least I had been. So in place of socializing, late office working filled the void of boredom, and a twice weekly meet up with Gregg, my lover, who had asked to marry me many times over.

The past reared its head again and an image of Nicki popped into my head out of nowhere and made my heart lurch. I closed my eyes to stop the floodgates of memories and tears, but it wasn't working.

'Lotti,' she'd say. 'One day we are both going to travel to America and make lots of money. We'll help the poor people and buy presents for children that have no toys.' Nicki was nine years old and had been sat on my bed when she had said that. She had always had a vision and maturity way beyond her years, and to this day, no one else has ever called me Lotti.

Nicki, my oldest friend and one of the few people who knew my secret - the person that I had distanced myself from since that very day that I had walked away. The memories had been too painful and a constant reminder so I had decided to make a fresh start and leave the past behind. I realized now that I had been wrong to cut her out of my life. She must have wondered what it was she'd done wrong and I felt that I needed her more than anyone else in the world right now, and I longed to pick the phone up and call her, but instead I threw back the last of the red wine from the glass and passed out on the bed.

CHAPTER 2

I stood on the deck as we headed back towards the harbour, feeling soothed by the rhythmic swaying of the boat.

The taste of salty spray on my lips from the Coral Sea took me back to my childhood and released memories that had been buried as deep as the ocean I was travelling across.

"Granddad!" I shouted. "Look, Granddad I caught a crab! Look!"

I was hopping up and down, pigtails flying in the flurry of activity. I was seven years old and even though it was summer in North East England I wore long trousers because there was a cold nip in the air once you got out to sea: according to my mother anyway. My jeans were covered in a mixture of bait, dirt and seawater. I held the wriggling crab by grabbing the back legs and holding the bottom part of the shell, so that the pincers could not snap at my fingers. My granddad had shown me this many times because most Sundays, weather depending, we went fishing in the North Sea in his trawler, the *Charlotte-Anne*, named after my great grandmother.

We never went too far out because my parents worried, so we usually stayed just outside of the bay so that we could still see people on the beach in the distance. We caught crabs in the pots that Granddad had set out the evening before, and while he hurled them up by hand I would sit patiently on my special seat and hang my mini crab pot over the side of the boat. My granddad would put bait in it for me and I would look out to sea, smelling the air and feeling lulled by the gentle rocking of the boat, until the line tugged at my fingers to tell me that a crab was trapped inside the pot. Sometimes it was hard to know when there was something in there and often I would yank the pot up in excited anticipation only to find it empty. "It's just the pull of the current, love," Granddad would say with a smile.

Granddad was a fisherman and he loved the sea. He always told me tales of the deep and I would sit enthralled by his big words and his rolling Northumbrian accent. Granddad was always dressed in black trousers held up by a pair of stretchy braces, and a casual shirt underneath and whether he was heading out to sea, popping for a pint, or going to a funeral, he was pretty much dressed the same, apart from swapping a pair of waders for shoes. He would show me pictures of Grandma sewing up holes in the fishing nets and crab pots, and pictures of her standing on the shore line, hurling the nets in. Mother would tell me that Grandma had been a hard worker and had endured a 'tough life'.

I would return home, hair all matted with salty seawater and burst through the door with tales of the ocean adventure I had just been on. Sometimes Dad would come with us but he usually got sea sick, so he preferred to stay at home.

"Never make a fisherman," Granddad would say as laughed and shook his head.

We would walk into the house between eleven thirty and twelve and the smell of a roast dinner cooking would tantalize my nostrils. There was always a crumble or suet pudding cooking alongside and we would sit after lunch, playing board games or watching television. Granddad lived with us since Grandma had died. I could barely remember Grandma because I had only been two years old when she had died. It was fun with Granddad because he always had time to tell me stories and he would say to me after each story, "Never forget, Charlotte, that every little girl is a princess and they deserve nothing less than a prince."

I shuddered as I remembered those words now.

Late afternoon, Mum would cook the crabs and I would play outside in the garden because I hated the way they tried to climb out of that huge metal pot. I loved the ocean, I loved eating seafood but I had always struggled with the way that crabs were cooked. I remember the first time I saw my mother put the crabs in the huge bubbling pot on the stove, I screamed as the crabs screamed and I sobbed uncontrollably, begging my mother to let them out. I still ate the sandwiches with gusto but to this day I still can't bear the thought of them being boiled in a pan.

We lived in a three-bedroom terraced house in a small fishing village called Alnmouth. It was approximately six kilometres south east of the bigger town of Alnwick, which was popular for its markets. Every Saturday we would go to the markets and my mother would buy fresh fish, fruit and vegetables. We would look at every stall even though they rarely differed from week to week and mostly consisted of homemade jams & baked goods, bric-a-brac stalls and local farmers' produce.

We would always stop off at a quaint little teashop aptly named 'The China Teapot'. My mother would drink hot sweet tea out of a china cup and I always had a biscuit or scone and a chocolate or strawberry milkshake. In the afternoon my father would take me to the beach and we would look for shells and straddle slimy green slippery rocks while looking in the pools of seawater for stranded fish. More often than not we would both return home with wet feet.

My mother was five foot five inches tall with long, dark, glossy hair and she had managed to keep her figure despite the enormous meals we ate as a family. My father was five foot eleven and like a big bear. His waistline continually grew and it always amazed me how my mother managed to stay so slim. While my mother was reserved and not a one to show affection through touch, my father would wrap his arms around me and ask how his favourite girl was when he came in from work.

My father worked at the plant, washing coal that came through from the local mines and he would leave for work at six am every morning and return at five pm every day, Monday to Friday.

Everyone knew each other in Alnmouth and wherever you went people would shout out and stop to talk to you, or help you with your shopping. Older people would ruffle the top of my hair and pinch my cheeks in a friendly way.

Guy Fawkes Night was a big event in the North East of England. Every year in the lead-up to the fifth of November, all of the local children would spend time after school, knocking on doors and asking for any old wood or papers. Most parents ended up with planks of wood and debris in their back yards in the weeks before November the fifth, much to their disdain.

Everyone felt excited on Guy Fawkes Day, and the end of the school day could not come quick enough. We would all take turns in gathering the wood for the bonfire and then one or two adults or older teens would build it as us younger ones helped carry smaller items, wincing as splinters dug into our skin. The fire would be lit after six pm, when it was dark and all of the parents and children were gathered around. There were designated houses that we would all take turns in visiting. Each house that took part would have a different treat waiting for the excited children: dipped toffee apples, hotdogs in buns, fresh biscuits and juice drinks. It was a wonderful atmosphere as everyone stood around the blazing bonfire, and it was a time that all of the neighbours made an effort to get together. Older children placed potatoes in the hot furnace of the fire and would only remove them once they were charcoal black and too hot to hold. It was common to see the teenagers with black soot all over their faces as they tried to eat the sizzling hot potatoes without burning their mouths. People would huddle round, chatting and savouring the feeling of skin heating up in the cold autumn air that left your breath hanging like a ghostly white mist. Rosy cheeked, we would watch the fire that was out of control, with angry red and orange flames licking out at anyone that dare to get too close, and we would wait until it calmed and became a molten mound of red glowing embers that threw out lazy bursts of grey messy ash.

Christmas was another occasion where everyone got together. I was an only child so I loved the attention of people calling in on Christmas morning to see what Santa had brought. Although we did not have any family in the immediate area, close friends of my parents and grandparents would call around for a Christmas drink and snack. I would get extra gifts of sweets and chocolate and Mum would be rushing around, flustered, as she made sure everyone had a drink in their hand, while also trying to prepare Christmas lunch. We all ate warm, homemade sweet mince pies dusted with icing sugar, and I was usually allowed a sip of Babycham with my Christmas lunch. Every year we ate the same thing: Turkey, stuffing, cranberry sauce, roast potatoes, mashed potatoes, Brussels sprouts, carrots, pigs in blankets and huge Yorkshire puddings all drowned in hot juicy gravy. Even though we felt fit to burst after lunch we somehow found room to eat a special dessert. My mother would head out to Marks and Spencer in the run up to Christmas, and she would remind us that once a year we were privy to a dessert from the 'posh' food store.

We would spend the next three days at least, eating our way through the remaining turkey until we were satiated, enough to last us almost another year.

We went on family holidays every August during the school holidays. Usually we travelled north to Berwick, Haggertson Castle, Kelso or Edinburgh. We would stay in a caravan park and I would have my own room with two small single beds in and not much room for anything else. Granddad would stay at home to look after the house and Pepper, my rabbit. I had named her Pepper because she was mostly white with speckles of black dotted on the edge of her fur. My mother had taken one look at her when dad brought her in and said, "Well I never. What a funny looking rabbit. You would think someone had sprinkled pepper on her." We had all laughed and the name just stuck.

There's something magical about staying in a caravan when you are a child. They have their own smell and even though they are fully equipped with a cooker, fridge and television, it almost felt like living in a real-life dolls' house where everything is smaller and more compact.

I would spend a lot of the holiday in the amusement arcades and lost count of how many two pence pieces I placed in the waterfall machine, which had rows and rows of money balancing, ready to drop at any second. Sometimes, if I was very lucky I would walk by and several coins would just drop into the metal cup as a vibration set them loose. I loved the noise of all the machines and the sounds of money steadily pumping out winnings for the lucky few. I spent hours watching the machines that had cuddly toys in and a huge claw hanging above, looking ready to grab one at every opportunity, but more often than not, the prize was lost on the last swing. I would nag my dad to win me a toy and despite his initial resistance, every holiday I came away with at least one and it was my most prized possession for the duration of the stay.

At Haggerston I always went horse riding. Parents could drop you off for an hour and you walked around and around the site on the back of a docile horse while one of the workers led you. The horses were very smelly and looking back, I'm sure they were very unhappy as they plodded on, resigned to their structured life. Nonetheless it was always the highlight of my holiday. My mother could never understand my obsession with horses. 'Stinking animals,' she'd say, and when I returned from horse riding she would insist I went in the shower and had a change of clothes. Every year I would beg them for a pony for Christmas and they would make soothing noises and talk about it needing a stable and the cost of hay. I still hoped every Christmas morning that somehow, a miracle would happen and I would unwrap a riding hat, boots and a saddle and then I would be taken outside where my very own pony would be standing, just waiting for me to wrap my arms around its neck. I picture myself plaiting its mane and grooming it until my arms ached. The little girl in me still longed for that pony to this day.

A sudden lurch of the boat as it hit an unexpected wave brought me back to the present and sent me toppling backwards and banging into another passenger.

"Sorry," I said as I pulled myself away from the old lady, who looked to be in her sixties and was brushing down her jacket as if to brush off the incident. "Not to worry, darl, no damage done," She replied briskly.

I excused myself and moved along the deck to a spot where the sea sprayed up. No one else wanted to stand there getting soaked but it suited me fine because I didn't feel like talking to anyone.

I stared back out to the ever-nearing coastline and for the first time in years I gave myself permission to drift into the black void of long ago.

CHAPTER 3

I stepped off the boat, relieved that the reef trip was over and I flopped onto the bed in the hotel room and lay staring at the ceiling. I was staying on Cairns esplanade in a nice hotel, situated directly opposite the beach, and set in amongst a long row of shops and restaurants.

I was exhausted after the six-hour boat trip but my mind was still too alert to go straight to sleep so I decided to have a quick shower and go out for some food.

I pulled on a pair of shorts and a short-sleeved top after freshening up and grabbed my handbag. It was April and still hot enough to wear shorts during the day and night. I decided against make-up but added a squirt of Chanel Coco – my one luxury that I'd refused to leave behind. My mobile lay switched off on the bedside cabinet, and although it was killing me not to have it, I was unsure how to go about dealing with the waves of emotion I felt when reading messages and listening to voice mails, so it stayed on the varnished wooden table like a ticking bomb, waiting for me to relent and bring it back to life.

I took a walk along the sea front until I found a restaurant that was busy enough to make me feel comfortable on my own, but quiet enough for me to think. I settled for a table outside a small seafood restaurant next to a bustling Italian, where alluring smells permeated the air. The restaurant overlooked the enormous lagoon, which was lit up at night with a fluorescent blue light that illuminated the whole area and helped set the ambiance. I ordered myself a bottle of Sauvignon Blanc, I intended to get drunk tonight because I knew at some stage I had to make a decision about where my life would go from here. The thought made me shudder and fear rolled in my stomach like thunder causing my hunger to suddenly disappear. I decided that I would eat later, but I ordered some tapas to keep the staff happy, and I sat back allowing my muscles to temporarily relax. It never ceased to amaze me how tense my muscles get when I am stressed out, I contemplated treating myself to a massage the following day.

I had arrived the previous night at nine pm after an eight-hour drive from Mackay. It had been a monotonous journey with a landscape that had barely changed from Townsville through to Cairns. Traffic had been steady and thankfully there had been no accidents to hold me up. The roads up north are far from great to travel on and consist of mainly single carriageway that is sporadically injected with an overtaking lane.

The further north I had travelled, the redder the soil and earth had become, and that was really the only defining feature between the two places because all of the bush and dry, dusty scrubland looked similar. Mountainous hills settled into the background all looking scarily analogous and it gave me a feeling that I had been driving on a running conveyor belt, not really moving or getting anywhere, had it not been for the odd wallaby or kangaroo breaking the scene, I would have thought it true.

I love Cairns. There's something about it that reminds me of the Spanish Islands, and that makes me think of home; but in a good way. It has a laid back, cool city vibe about it. People are friendly and there are lots of restaurants and shops with just the right amount of hustle and bustle. No matter what night of the week you head out to eat, the restaurants are busy enough for people to take no notice of a woman sat by herself and that is a real bonus for me, especially tonight because the last thing I feel like is company.

I watch people as I sit, envious of their normality. So oblivious to other people's suffering, as they laugh and chat excitedly while taking photographs without a care in the world. It's an awful feeling when you're fighting an internal battle because you suddenly become envious of those who aren't.

Out of nowhere a surge of anger rises up and I have a sudden urge to yell, "Make the most of it, because you never know when your life will change!" In particular I feel annoyed with the large woman sat two tables along who clearly enjoys being the centre of attention and has the most annoying guffaw of a laugh.

To silence my thoughts I opt for a large gulp of cool, crisp white wine to sooth my fractious, jumpy mind. Not the answer, I know, but anything to calm and numb my mind right now has to be a good thing, I tell myself.

I order a calamari salad because I can feel the wine flowing too quickly through my veins and I decide it's probably a good idea to eat before I keel over. I know I have lost weight this past week because my clothes are loose. I order more wine and the petite brunette waitress smiles sweetly as she returns with a fresh ice bucket to keep it cool. I drain the last out of the first bottle and asked her to take the empty away. It's not a good look when you're sat at a table surrounded by empty bottles when you're on your own. She's very professional and acts as if it is perfectly normal for a woman to be drowning herself in alcohol while all alone on a Saturday night.

I am aware of a pair of eyes on me and try to ignore them but no matter which way I look I can feel the stare penetrating through me, burning a hole in my skin.

Eventually tired of the game of avoidance, I turn to the next table and to where the burning look is coming from. The old lady that I had almost knocked over on the boat is sat staring at me. She nods.

"You managed to knock anybody else over?"

Before I can answer she's off again.

"Here by yourself then, are you? Me too." She mutters and I wonder if she's talking to me, or to herself.

"Looks that way," I reply a little too sharply, and as soon as the words leave my mouth I regret it.

"Sorry, that was rude of me, it's just been a long day. In fact if I'm honest it's probably been one of the longest weeks of my life, and believe me, that's some achievement."

The words burst out of my mouth before I can stop them and I decide that the wine has definitely loosened my tongue because I am not usually compelled to tell complete strangers about my life.

I sigh and take another gulp and before I can stop her, she has moved herself over to my table and informed the waitress that she would like her food and another whisky delivered to my, sorry, to *our* table.

"Could do with some company. The name's Margie." She smiles a crooked smile, revealing missing teeth and then shoves her weathered hand into mine and shakes it roughly, almost manlike, before shuffling her chair and dropping her handbag on the floor.

She talks quietly under her breath while making herself comfortable, and despite my initial reluctance I can't help but smile at this pushy old woman sat at the table, sipping her whisky on the rocks.

"Nice to meet you. I'm Charlotte," I say, smiling despite my initial annoyance at my peace being shattered.

"So what brings you here, Charlotte? You're not an Aussie, so are you travelling? Recently divorced, is that it?"

Wow, I think. I hope this is not going to be an interrogation all night long, so I try to answer as many questions as possible when I reply.

"I've lived here for almost four years. I'm single, although I do kind of have a 'someone', and I work and live in Brisbane as CEO of a company. What about you?"

"Still hanging on to that pommy accent I see. I have no idea what a CEO is but it sounds good. I have travelled from Victoria, live in a small place called Beaufort. Nice place, quiet, with not many people, but once a year I like to travel somewhere I've not been before. My husband died five years ago and it's pretty much all I have to look forward to at my age. He always wanted to come to Cairns but never made it, poor old bugger. I have a son who's forty-two but he lives in America and I'm not much good with this technology lark so I don't use a computer. He asks me when he phones if I will Skype him but it's too new-fangled for an oldie like meself. You got kids, Charlotte?"

I freeze momentarily, unprepared for that question. Thankfully, the universe steps in and saves me as a bell chimes from the food hatch and the waitress whisks our meals off the counter and walks quickly towards us.

We eat mostly in silence, but strangely enough it feels comfortable, almost as if I have known Margie for a lifetime.

On finishing I sit back, soaking up the warmth of the night and the laid back atmosphere. The bars and restaurants are still lively and people are walking, huddled in groups, faces flushed from alcohol and laughter.

We chat for and while and Margie asks me lots of questions about England. A sudden wave of exhaustion hits me just before eleven thirty, so I thank her for her company, and stand to leave.

"Have you got far to walk?" She asks with a slight slur to her words and a pleading look in her eye. The whisky has obviously got to her and I assume that she wants a chaperone back to her hotel.

"Would you like me to walk with you to your hotel, Margie?"

"That would be lovely, darl. Why don't we walk along the esplanade, it's quieter there and I like the sound of the sea and it's a rare thing for me to be out this late at night, so a walk will be nice."

I love the way Australians abbreviate everything. Darling became darl, ambulance is an ambo, fire fighters are fireies.

Margie held onto me by looping her arm through mine and I admired this sassy sixty four year old woman who had travelled all this way on her own without a hint of self-doubt. It was hard not to like her.

We walked along in the cool night air, wind blowing gently as we listened to the waves lapping up against the wooden pier, swirling beneath in a gentle, hypnotic rhythm.

We sit down on a wooden bench that faces out to sea, and all we can see is the blackness of the night with the occasional light in the far distance. The sky is clear and splattered with thousands of stars no bigger than a pinprick. It feels so good to be surrounded by nothing but the black of the night and an old woman who I barely know.

There's definitely something cathartic about talking to strangers. Maybe it's because you don't think you'll ever see them again, so you kind of let go of all the pretence, and in my case I guess two bottles of wine had helped as well!

I start talking about Joe, aware that once I open my mouth I would have little control over what came out. It had been building for a while now and as much as I favoured denial and burial of my memories, there is only so far you can go before your body or mind takes over and does what it needs to. In my case, at this moment in time, I needed to talk.

****

I was sixteen years old and out on my first date. Joe was nineteen and he had black hair and the bluest eyes I had ever seen. I used to laugh to Nicki and say that those eyes had hypnotized me the first time I looked into them.

Nicki was my best friend and we had been pretty much inseparable since primary school. We lived one street away from each other and spent most Saturdays together and often went around to each other's houses to hang out after school. We did gymnastics together, and then trampoline, and when we got bored of that, we went to roller discos and danced to Boyzone in our bedrooms and stared at posters of Ronan Keating. Eventually, as we grew, gymnastics faded out in favour of fashion, music and make-up. Followed shortly after by boys.

Joe Porter had become friends with Nicki's brother Will, and I had met him a few weeks previously when he had walked into Nicki's house with Will after a football match, all rugged, flushed and dirty. I had been too embarrassed to talk to him though and had muttered a quick, 'Hello,' before running up to Nicki's room and quietly squealing in excitement that he had even spoke to me. Joe was fairly new to the area from what Nicki told me. Apparently he had moved from down south with his parents and apart from that, no one seemed to know much about the family. He came across as very confident and I guess I was in awe of him because he seemed so sure of whom he was, and what he was about and that was the complete opposite of who I was. He had asked me out on a date the second time I saw him at Nicki's house and I almost passed out. He was so good looking and I couldn't believe that someone like him would be interested in me.

I had dark hair that was shoulder length and naturally wavy. I was in the awkward stage of blossoming from teenager to woman and I had a shape like my mother's with a natural curve at my waistline. People would comment on my figure but I never really thought of myself as attractive, I guess I was just me, and I didn't pay much attention to how I looked.

Joe was a mechanic at the local garage and seemed popular with the guys that he worked with and played football with. They all usually headed to the pub on a Saturday or Sunday afternoon to watch the football or relax after a match and sometimes Nicki and I hung around deliberately, hoping to catch them leaving the pub. One or two of them would wolf whistle and although we would never turned around, we would smile like Cheshire cats, and giggle to each other as we walked along, trying a little too hard to be cool. We could hear Will giving whoever it was an earful, clearly unimpressed that his friends thought of his sister in that way.

It was a Friday night on the third of July and I was on my first date with Joe. He pulled up in his shiny black saloon car and my heart was beating as fast as it would if I had just ran a marathon. I felt very grown up slipping into the passenger seat beside him and also, extremely nervous at the same time. I worried that he would find me boring so I spent most of the night listening to him and answering questions that he asked me. He told me that as soon as I was old enough to drink alcohol, he would take me out to Alnwick for a night out and my stomach flipped when he said this, because it implied that we would be seeing each other again.

I had worried all day long about him wanting to kiss me because I'd not really kissed anyone before, unless you counted kiss chase when I was about nine years old. I'd brushed my teeth until my gums hurt and gargled mouthwash just in case the occasion arose, and, much to my delight, it did. As we parked at the top of my lane, out of sight of my house, Joe leant in and kissed me gently on the lips. I was still reeling from that when he went in for a full passionate kiss. He whispered something faintly after our lips parted and I could have sworn I heard the word 'gorgeous'; so I allowed it to hang in the air, twinkling above me, and I savoured the feeling of euphoria; a feeling I had never experienced before, and one that soon became like a drug to me.

Every day Joe would text me and ask how my day was going. He would pick me up from work and I have to admit that I felt secretly pleased with myself when some of the girls I worked with told me how lucky I was to have him as a boyfriend.

I worked in a small local upholstery business and I was in admin along with another six girls. My job was to book people in for fittings and measurement for whatever they were needing, (sofa covers, curtains etc.) and deal with invoices. I had secured the job straight from school and considered myself lucky to get a full time, job so quickly at such a young age.

I continued to see Joe but after a while, Nicki started complaining about the amount of time I was spending with him, and it became a bit of an issue between the three of us. I made the mistake of telling Joe how she felt and he accused her of being selfish and jealous of me, while Nicki felt that Joe was too intense and wouldn't allow me breathing space. I tried hard to please them both, but more often than not I would end up sneaking to Nicki's house, because Joe was so in love with me that he told me he couldn't stand to be apart for more than twenty four hours.

For the first time in my life I felt an all-consuming need to be with the man I loved. If I was not with Joe, I thought about him constantly and I would smile to myself as I replayed conversations in my head, as I closed my eyes and pictured his perfect face. I used to imagine myself walking down the aisle and mini Joes running around our house. He was my entire life and I didn't care that he resented us spending time apart: I knew it was because he loved me and I felt the same. We laughed so much and he was so good to be around.

Slowly Nicki and I kept in touch less and less, as Joe and I spent more and more time together.

On my seventeenth birthday Joe bought me a watch and on the back he had inscribed, 'Love you always. Joe'.

Two days later we stood around the bonfire and talked about the future, about our future. Joe wanted to travel the world and we talked about skiing in Canada, hiring a Harley Davidson and driving down Route Sixty-six in America, and going to the midnight zoo in Singapore. There was so much to look forward to and I felt as if it was all too good to be true. *I know now that it was!*

Joe was very protective and liked to know where I was and whom I was with. He told me that it was because he loved me so much and if I was honest, it felt good to know that someone loved me like that, and because I'd never had a boyfriend prior to him, I just assumed that it was a normal part of every relationship and I never questioned his jealousy or possessiveness.

However, there was one thing that bothered me about Joe, even though I believed that time would change his views. He would tell me regularly that he never wanted children and I just assumed that he would change his mind once we settled down and married. I mean, don't most nineteen year olds say the same thing? Whenever he asked me what my views were on children I would say, 'What will be will be,' which was a favourite saying of my mother's. The reality, of course, was that I hoped to have children someday. In fact I wanted two children with not too much of an age gap, but firstly I wanted a few years to enjoy married life and travel a little before committing to motherhood. I was certain that once we had ticked our travel goals off the list of to-dos, children would definitely be the next step in our relationship.

The day before Christmas Eve, my granddad died in his sleep, from a heart attack at the age of seventy-two. I was heartbroken. Joe held me in his arms and told me that he would protect me from everything he possibly could, and if he couldn't, he would wipe my tears away and love me even more. I was so in love with him and could not imagine my life without him.

Christmas day was a quiet affair because we were still coming to terms with Granddad's death. Joe came around for tea and I was pleased because it broke the silence that sat awkwardly between us. My mother kept crying and leaving the room. Dad tried to comfort her, but she would pretend that she was fine.

We left the house after we'd eaten and we drove around for an hour with the music blasting while we sat freezing in the car, trying to make smoke rings with our frosty breath and I wished that I could freeze these innocent precious times that were so full of happiness.

Joe stayed strong for me over the following months as my family adjusted to life without my granddad. The house felt so empty and Sundays were never the same after his death.

My parents accepted Joe as he was quite the charmer and he definitely won my mother over, by flashing his pearly white smile and complimenting her cooking with a cheeky wink. "You could do a lot worse than that boy, I'll tell you, Charlotte. Make sure you hold on to him," she would say, reinforcing the fact that I was lucky to have him. Joe would talk about football with my dad, and they would sometimes share a pint at the pub if he was staying for Sunday lunch, which was becoming more frequent now.

I was doing quite well at work and had received a pay rise, so I started secretly saving for a house. I dreamt about living with Joe and I would picture myself ironing his clothes and cooking his favourite meal of steak, chips and mushrooms. I imagined him sweeping me up in his arms and kissing me when he came in from work, swinging me around, both of us laughing, and I pictured us curled up on the sofa, flicking through travel brochures in front of a crackling fire, with candles burning around the room giving off a romantic hue. I desperately wanted it to happen and saved every spare penny that I had.

I had met Joe's parents only briefly, a few times, because they were travelling back and forward between Alnmouth and Surrey. His mum didn't work and his dad was self-employed and semi-retired with someone running the bulk of his plumbing company for him. I could never quite understand why they had moved away from their friends and family at such a late stage in their life but they never talked about it and it felt rude to bring the subject up, so I said nothing. Both of Joe's parents were quiet and very polite, but I detected from the onset that Joe seemed to have a strained relationship with them. I couldn't quite put my finger on what the problem was but there was a definite tension. Joe refused to talk about his parents if I asked, so it became a bit of a touchy subject and I just accepted their relationship for what it was.

Joe's grandma, who was eighty years old, had fallen and broken her hip and was currently in a rehabilitation unit waiting to return home, so his parents had decided that they would move in with her until she was well enough to look after herself. They returned to Surrey and Joe was left in charge of the house.

It was there that we had sex for the first time.

I was a virgin and although Joe had never told me whether he was or not, he certainly came across as confident and experienced. He had been quite good about *not going all the way* and had never pressured me to have sex, but I saw the frustration in his face when I said I wasn't ready, and he would always be off with me for a day or two afterwards. He would apologize and say it was because I was *so damn sexy* and that it was driving him crazy and I would feel flattered. I desperately wanted to keep him happy so it felt like the right thing to do, having sex.

I was so nervous the first time, but Joe was reassuring and loving. He used a condom and suggested that I go on the pill as he didn't want any accidents happening. It felt so right to be with him and I couldn't picture my life without him, and after we had made love I felt as if I had signed a silent binding contract with him, and it felt fantastic.

Life ticked along happily, although looking back, the nearer it got to my eighteenth birthday, the more insecure and edgy Joe seemed to get. He started asking me questions about whether I thought it was appropriate for women to go out drinking with work colleagues or friends, and I told him that every Friday the girls from work went out for a few drinks and that they were looking forward to my eighteenth birthday so they could take me along with them. Joe told me that once a woman was spoken for, she should stay at home with her husband-to-be and look after him. I had laughed, unsure if he was joking, but he did not join in with my laughter: nor did he speak much for the rest of that night. I had the feeling that I had done something wrong and went to bed feeling confused and anxious. I slept badly that night, trying to figure out what the problem could be. I hated when Joe got like this because I would spend hours analysing everything, wondering how I could have upset him.

One week later, over dinner at a local restaurant, the week before my eighteenth birthday, Joe proposed.

We were eating at our favourite restaurant Delrosa's when he dropped to one knee straight after desert.

"Charlotte Jackson, I love you more every day and I want to spend the rest of my life with you. Will you marry me?"

Oh, my god, I was thinking as I sat, stunned, tears ready to spill down my face. Joe looked so handsome and desperately nervous as he stayed on one knee waiting on my reply, beckoning for an answer with his hypnotic blue eyes.

"Yes. Yes!" I had said as tears of happiness streamed down my cheeks.

The restaurant erupted into rounds of applause and wolf whistles and we received a complimentary bottle of champagne.

My ring was a square cut diamond solitaire and I cried more tears of joy as Joe slipped the ring onto my finger.

The following day, Joe told me that it wasn't a good idea to go out after work on a Friday because I was engaged and we were now saving up for a house.

****

My eighteenth birthday was spent in York. Joe had booked a five star hotel and we spent the day walking the cobbled streets, soaking up the atmosphere, and the night was spent eating food, drinking cocktails and making love. It was perfect: almost too perfect, looking back.

As the months passed he showered me with love and affection, but he also had a tendency to fly off the handle about the smallest of things. Joe was very jealous but he assured me it was because he loved me so much and told me that once we were married he would feel more secure. I loved that Joe loved me so much, but at times it did feel claustrophobic. Like him, though, I was certain that things would change once we were married.

Joe told me on several occasions that I could not trust any man because they would 'want in my knickers'. I felt shocked and a little embarrassed as he ranted about men having hidden agendas and how women and men could never be just friends so it wasn't a good idea to speak to men. A feeling of unease would settle over me every time he went off like that, and I was never sure how best to respond, so I would wait patiently until he had calmed down. I had learnt that if I tried to discuss anything with him, he would storm off in a mood and refuse to answer my calls or answer the door. He was always full of apologies and reassurances that everything he did was out of love for me and that I needed to accept that he was a passionate man, who loved me very much.

We set the wedding date for April because Joe was desperate to get married, so it would be a short engagement. My mum was frantic at not having time to plan an elaborate wedding for her only daughter, but I went along with what Joe wanted because he seemed so eager to get married, and as long as he was happy, I was happy.

I asked Nicki to be my chief bridesmaid and even though things were fine between us, I knew deep down that she didn't like Joe and I knew that the feeling was mutual. She blamed him for the change in our relationship. However, she managed to put aside all doubts so that she could help plan the arrangements.

47

I had decided to have a small hen party at my mum's, because Joe disliked the typical hen parties that came to town. He told me that they were trashy and sleazy and only common women went out with handcuffs and condoms hanging off a veil.

I wanted a traditional, old-fashioned wedding and I chose a white silk wedding dress with an embroidered pearl and diamanté fitted bodice, with sweetheart neckline and full skirt. My veil was splattered with crystals that twinkled in the sunlight and I felt like a princess, and I knew that my Grandad would be looking down on me.

I had Nicki as my chief bridesmaid, as well as my two younger cousins, Helen and Scarlett. The girls all wore maroon coloured strapless dresses with a posy of white and black baccara roses, which complemented their dresses beautifully, and the three of them giggled nervously awaiting their duties.

I remember my father turning to me on my wedding morning with tears in his eyes.

"You look beautiful, Charlotte. Joe is one hell of a lucky man to have you. How do you feel? Are you sure this is what you want? It's never too late to back out, you know." He'd said softly. I had soothed him and assured him that I was the lucky one and that it was what I wanted more than anything in the whole wide world. Looking back, I often wonder if he had a sixth sense for what would happen in the not too distant future.

The photographs were so beautiful. The contrast of my white dress against the bridesmaids' maroon dresses and flowers: it was simply stunning and such a perfect day.

I turned to look at Margie, who was sat there, listening intently.

She smiled and nodded as if to give me permission to continue.

"My family travelled from Scarborough. Mum's sister, Aunt Trish, and Uncle Tommy and their daughters Helen and Scarlett, who were my bridesmaids. Dad's sister Susan lived in Australia and she couldn't make it. She was fifty-two and married but she had never had children. We spoke occasionally on the telephone, usually at Christmas, but I hadn't seen her since I was very young. She did send a wedding card and an invitation for us to visit anytime we felt like being adventurous which was very nice of her, and that is how I come to be sitting here today, but I'll get to that part soon!

Joe's parents, Gloria and Tom, travelled from Surrey but sadly, his grandma couldn't make such a long journey. She was out of the convalescent home but still in pain and unable to walk far. They had arranged some home support for her while they attended the wedding, but they were leaving the following morning. Dad's best friend Jimmy travelled from Scotland and surprised Dad, which made his day even more special.

We were married on a sunny day in April in the local church, St John the Baptist's. It was a perfect day. All of the guests turned up, the weather was beautiful, the food was fantastic and the atmosphere was relaxed. Picturing the photographs in my head, we looked so happy and so excited for our future.

We enjoyed a reception at the local masonic hall and had a live band and disco for the evening reception, which most of Alnmouth attended. We had asked people for gift cards as presents because we didn't really have anywhere to store anything and we wanted to decide on a colour scheme once we got around to buying a house.

And so, after being a relationship with Joe for two years, on the seventeenth of April two thousand and ten I became Mrs Charlotte Porter at the young age of eighteen.

We had a ten-day honeymoon in a private villa in Cyprus, courtesy of my parents. We ate out at Cypriot restaurants, drank wine while we watched the sun set, and we explored the sights on the days when it was too hot to lie around the pool. I really felt like the luckiest girl alive.

No one who was at that wedding could have predicted what lay ahead! Least of all me!

CHAPTER 4

Joe felt that it was best to live at his parents' house for a few months after our wedding so that we could save more money for a house of our own. We already had a good deposit but he had set his heart on one of the stone built houses that overlooked the River Aln. His motto was if you're going to buy a house, buy a house that you would want to spend the rest of your life in. I agreed with his philosophy but worried about making such a big commitment.

We returned from our honeymoon and moved straight in, and if I'm honest, I felt like a visitor in the house and found it hard to relax, despite his parents not being there. I hoped that we didn't have to stay too long so I tried encouraging Joe to look at cheaper houses, but he had his mind set on the house with the big price tag and he wasn't budging.

Joe's mood changed almost as soon as we returned home from honeymoon. He complained if I arranged to meet up with Nicki and accused me of not wanting to spend time with him. I told him he was being silly but he would get so moody that it almost wasn't worth the trouble, so I usually ended up meeting with her when he played football, but it always felt rushed and time limited.

Nicki would say things like:

"I can't believe that you aren't allowed to go out with your friends. How old fashioned is he? He must think because he has a ring on your finger that he owns you now."

I would feel torn when she talked like that. Part of me wanted to defend Joe and part of me wanted to agree with Nicki. She didn't understand, though. When things were good I could not have asked for more, but when Joe was moody and refusing to speak to me it made me feel ill. My stomach would churn, I lost my appetite and I just wanted the awful feeling of dread to leave my body and I would end up begging him to speak to me or forgive me, even when he had started it, simply because it was torture living in the same house as him and not communicating. I hated feeling as if I was being punished for something, especially if I didn't know what I was being punished for!

Joe was against me going out with the girls on a Friday night because he told me it made me look available, and I was now a married woman and needed to start acting like one. He would then cuddle up to me and kiss my neck, sending shivers down my spine before promising me a night I would never forget if I stayed in with him. He would hug me tight until I felt suffocated and tell me how much he loved me and that he would never let me leave him. I could never understand why he would say that, as I could not envisage my life without him. Sometimes - well, quite often if I'm honest - he left me feeling very confused.

Eventually the girls at work stopped asking me to go out, as did Nicki and other girls I had grown up with. It was just Joe and I against the world.

****

After a few months of married life, Joe started going out for a drink after work. He would tell me that he would be home for six o'clock, but more often than not it was nearer eight or nine o'clock. I would feel annoyed as I sat in the house waiting; yet I knew if I went out he would be annoyed. One night we had a huge argument about it when he came in. He kissed me on the cheek and headed straight to the fridge for a beer. I thought I would test the waters by telling him that I was going out the following Friday with the girls from work.

He sneered.

"Looking for cock more like, because that's what those little sluts do. I've seen them laughing, giggling and flirting with men. You want to go out with them, that's fine. Just don't expect me to come home that night."

My heart lurched and I was left speechless. I sat and wondered how we'd gone from A-Z in the blink of an eye. I couldn't believe that he would be so extreme but I certainly didn't want to test him out, so needless to say, I refused the invite.

Next morning Joe suggested that we go out together on the Saturday night.

Saturday came and I had booked into the hairdressers to get my hair curled. I was going to make a huge effort so I booked in for a manicure afterwards and I'd bought myself a new, fitted black dress. Joe had gone to the pub for a game of pool so it gave me some breathing space to get ready and get in the mood.

I had the music pumping when he walked upstairs as I was just putting the finishing touches to my make-up. He walked into the bedroom as I smoothed my dress down and turned to him. For once I felt as if I looked lovely, my dress fitted like a glove and the extra effort I'd made had boosted my confidence. I beamed at Joe, waiting for his compliment.

"You're not going out looking like that," he spat, before laughing. "And what the fuck have you done to your hair?"

Joe walked downstairs, laughing to himself, getting louder with each step that he descended.

I felt as if everything inside of my body had drained out of me in one split second. I sat on the bed and cried and questioned if I really look that bad? Bad enough that my own husband would laugh at me?

I started doubting myself, and my judgment. I had felt so nice all dressed up, and now I didn't even want to leave the house. I heard Joe coming back up the stairs so I tried to dry my eyes.

"Don't turn the waterworks on the minute I say something you don't like. You know me Char, I'm honest if nothing else, and if you look a mess I'm fucking well going to tell you. I'm not having you walk in the pub and have people laugh at you. Now go and wash your face and do something with your hair, for fuck's sake. I'll see what's in your wardrobe and then we'll go to the pub."

I really didn't feel like going out but I knew if I didn't I'd be accused of being boring, so I plugged my straighteners in and reapplied my make-up.

Joe was standing with a pair of black trousers and a camisole top. The outfit was very plain and understated, but I'd rather that than have him make fun of me.

We walked into the pub thirty minutes later and people nodded, stuck a hand up and said hello. We found a table in a quiet corner and sat down. Joe was chatting away as if nothing happened and everything was fine until two older men sat down near us. I noticed them looking at me, so I did my best to avoid making any eye contact so as not to upset Joe, he didn't like it if I looked at men because he said I had eyes that gave people the come on. I waited as long as I could before going to the toilet, self-conscious as I passed them.

I was aware that they both looked at me and followed me with their eyes and I heard them talking but couldn't quite make out what they were saying. I hoped they weren't laughing at me.

When I returned to my seat Joe looked annoyed.

"You see them two over there," he said, nodding in their direction. "Did you see them staring at you? Do you want to know what they said?"

His eyes looked black and his face was scarily taut as he stared at me, making me feel nervous.

I didn't answer but chose to look down in the hope that he would change the subject. I felt the anger oozing out of his pores and it made me feel uneasy.

"Do you know when someone is that ugly that you have to look at them twice? You do know what I mean, don't you, Charlotte? You look, and then look again. Well, they said that you were that ugly that they couldn't stop looking at you. Cheeky bastards, I've got a good mind to go over there and smack them one."

I felt sick and my head started to spin. I felt as if my world and everything in it was becoming foreign to me. I was already feeling fragile after the comments about my hair and outfit and now this. Why would someone be so cruel as to call me ugly? I looked at Joe and his handsome face and I suddenly felt so inferior. I'd never really valued myself or thought myself good looking but being defined as ugly was beyond soul destroying.

"Lucky you've got me, eh, Charlotte," he said with a wink as if he was able to read my mind. He sauntered to the bar with a confident swagger and a smile on his face and I sat surrounded by my confusion and heightened paranoia.

And so the cycle continued, with Joe being loving and attentive one minute, promising me the earth, and then putting me down the next. As the weeks turned into months, I felt my confidence drain out of me like a slow trickling hour-glass. I hung on to every compliment that he gave me and cried at every hurtful word the shot out of his mouth. More often than not it was the latter. He was becoming very good at telling me what I was useless at, or how unattractive I was becoming.

The only time that I felt carefree and happy was when he was in a good mood and talking about our future. However, this would usually be followed by a pattern of him dropping hints about 'marrying too young' and sometimes he made me wonder if he was about to up and leave. He seemed to take pleasure from telling me regularly that he'd had enough and I was never quite sure what he'd had enough of because it felt as if he changed his mind and moods as often as the weather. The goal-posts changed daily and what would make him laugh one day seemed to piss him off the next. It was exhausting, but my love for him was so strong I put up with his mood swings and tried to judge his moods on a daily basis and avoid triggers that might set him off.

It was hard work and I permanently felt drained, but if Joe was happy, then I was happy, and people always said that marriage takes work.

CHAPTER 5

There were three significant changes to come in my life and the first one happened twelve weeks and three days after our wedding day.

My parents were on their way to visit my Aunt Trish, my mum's sister who lived in Scarborough. They were driving along the A1M on a rainy, windy day, when a lorry that was overtaking them lost control and crashed into them, causing a pile up involving six cars. Five people lost their life that day. My parents, and a woman and her two children, aged five and three.

When I opened the door to two police officers, my first reaction was to think that they had the wrong address. I smiled and then my heart lurched and ice ran through my veins as they said my name. My first thought was of Joe. I could feel the colour drain out of me as I led them into the sitting room.

As they told me the tragic news about my parents' deaths I was aware of someone screaming. I felt removed from my body and it was only when one of the officers placed an arm around my shoulder that I felt myself snap back into reality, and I realized that the person screaming had been me.

I was numb and I couldn't think. I felt as if a heavy weight was crushing my chest and my breathing felt laboured.

Joe came running into the house. He had seen the police car outside and had panicked. I tried to tell him what had happened through gulping sobs and short, gasping breaths but I could not get the words out. His face was pale and I could see that he was visibly shaken at the state that I was in. The dark haired officer took him to one side and told him the news. For a minute he stood stock still, paralysed, and then he picked up the phone and called my doctor, explaining what had happened and asked him to come out to the house to give me something to help me with the shock.

I was still oscillating between gasping short breaths and shuddering sobs when Dr. Walter walked in. He was an elderly man but appeared to never have aged since I was about five years old. He took my hand in his and tenderly rubbed it while offering his condolences at my loss. He told me that he was writing out a prescription for some diazepam and that I should take the tablets whenever needed over the course of the next few days, to help with the shock.

He placed the prescription on the table near the door and as he left a gust of cold autumn wind blew in and sent it fluttering onto the floor. I remember staring at it for what seemed like a lifetime. Joe picked up the prescription and kissed my forehead.

"Go upstairs and lie down, Char. I'll only be five minutes and then you can have one of the tablets and have a sleep while I sort things out."

The police officers left and it was agreed that Joe would formally identify the bodies. I was in no state to even think about it.

Oh, God, I felt so sick and my heart rate was doing its best to run a marathon even though I was only climbing the stairs. I lay on the bed. The bed that had seemed so normal half an hour ago, but now, now it just seemed foreign. I felt as if I was swimming in air. Everything looked different and everything felt wrong somehow. My whole life would never be the same ever again. I started sobbing: huge racking sobs that hurt my body but still somehow managed to allow the aching heartbreak to seep through. I felt weak and scared. Scared that my life could be turned upside down so quickly.

Joe walked through the bedroom door.

"Baby, come here, oh, Char." He hugged me to him until I thought I would pass out through lack of air.

He kissed the top of my head as I clung to him and cried myself dizzy. Exhausted, I lay on the bed, took a diazepam and closed my swollen, gritty eyes. I wanted to black out and erase this horrific day. I wanted to wake up and find that everything was just as it had been. I drifted into a foggy land of emptiness while my husband took on the grim job of looking at my dead parents in a morgue.

I woke to find Joe sitting on the bed, stroking my hair. I felt dazed and confused. Unsure if it was morning or night. I was hot and sweaty and wondered if a fever had caused me to have a nightmare.

I sat up and looked at him.

"Did I dream it?' Did … was -" I couldn't get the words out, but I didn't need to.

Joe looked at me and a pained expression slipped over his face like a mask as he shook his head, confirming that it was true. I felt my heart rate increase again and the breath leave my body.

"I'm so sorry, Char baby. I wish there was something I could do for you," he replied as he cradled me in his arms.

And so it began, the days of my husband being a rock and taking care of me. Making me eat when I didn't have an appetite. Taking me out when I wanted to stay indoors.

"You can't lock yourself away," he'd say. "You've got to eat, Char, or you'll waste away."

I truly had no idea how to even go about organising a funeral. Joe went through the papers in my parents' house and found that they were insured through Co-op Funerals. They had also bought themselves an allocated space for their ashes. I was astounded at their organization and disgusted at my naivety. I suppose it's not often an eighteen year old girl buries her parents together on the same day though and until death hits you, you always assume that it's too far into the future to worry about it.

The next few days passed in a haze of medication and a blur of activity, with friends calling in every few hours and neighbours bringing food around. Although it was lovely, I just wanted to lie on my bed and stare into space, or sleep. I felt physically exhausted and struggled to stay awake all day. Dr. Walter called in to ask me how I was doing and when I explained how I felt, he assured me that I was still in shock and to rest when my body told me to.

The vicar came around to ask me what kind of service I wanted for my parents. They had made it clear in their funeral package that they both wanted to be cremated and their ashes would be placed in the same urn and then sealed into a special commemorative wall inside the graveyard.

Luckily the vicar knew my parents well because they went to church every Sunday, so he had plenty of stories to relay and people to relate them to. The service would be held in two days' time at the same church that I was married in only thirteen weeks earlier.

Dad's best friend, Jimmy, had asked to do a eulogy and I was more than happy for other people to step in and take over catering. The less I had to do the better.

I still felt numb and could not shake the feeling of foggy exhaustion and nausea that clung to me like dirt.

The following day I struggled to do much and walked from room to room trying to make sense of my life and the reality of being alone. Nicki was travelling overseas with her family and I had no way of getting in touch with her and by the time she returned from her holiday, the funeral would be over and done with.

****

It was Tuesday and Joe always played football and then went out for a few beers with his friends. He insisted that he would stay in but I convinced him that I would have a bath and an early night. I thought it would do him good to get out for a while and get away from my depressing mood.

I had run the bath and was just about to undress when there was a knock at the door.

"Charlotte, it's Jimmy, love. Are you there?"

Jimmy had been my dad's best friend since childhood and he had moved from Alnmouth to Glasgow in Scotland six years ago because of work.

Jimmy was standing in the doorway with his son, Graham, who was my age. It was so good to see the two of them and I immediately burst into tears. They both hugged me and we made our way into the living room.

"Charlotte, I'm so sorry, my darling. I'm still in shock myself so I can't imagine how you are feeling."

Jimmy wiped a stray tear from his eye. "I hope you don't mind but I brought round a few beers. Thought I'd drink to your dad's memory. Do you mind, love?"

"Not at all. It's so lovely to see you both. I know we didn't get a chance to talk much at the wedding but I'm so pleased you're here now. Joe is out playing five a side and then he'll go for a drink with the boys, but he should be in for nine."

The boys opened their beers and I had a glass of wine. It wasn't often I drank in the house but I felt that I needed it tonight. Jimmy chatted about my dad and I even managed to laugh at the memory of him hanging over the side of the boat when we had all gone out to sea. I also cried a lot.

Jimmy decided to leave at eight thirty. "I've had a long drive love and to be honest I'm still getting my head around it all, so you'll have to excuse me."

I suddenly felt panicky at the thought of being alone.

"Graham, you'll stay, won't you? Please. I could do with the company and you can tell me about work or … I don't know, anything I guess. Just to try and take my mind off everything. Plus I really want you to meet Joe."

Jimmy hugged me and told me that he would call around tomorrow and Graham opened himself another beer. I topped up my glass and had to admit that I felt a little tipsy. I hadn't had much to eat and although I'd not had any of the tablets off the doctor, I hadn't slept well the night before.

Graham was telling me about his job as an IT consultant when Joe came through the door, bringing the cold night air with him.

"Babe, I'll just have a quick shower and then I'll come see you," he shouted. He ran up the stairs into the bathroom and then into our bedroom. I could hear him running back over the floor boards and down the stairs two at a time.

"Char, where are -" He opened the door, concern etched all over his face.

"In here, Joe," I said.

"The bath. I was worried, the water was still in and, well -"

Awkwardness hung in the air like visible smoke when he realized I was not alone. He looked at Graham and then at me. Joe had met Graham at the wedding but he probably couldn't remember him considering how many people were there. His face was set and he was clearly not happy. Graham seemed not to notice and stood up to shake his hand. "Joe, nice to meet you again. I grew up with Charlotte and my dad and her dad were good friends. Dad just left, and we were having a catch up. Do you fancy a beer?"

"Thanks, I will," he said oddly.

The next hour passed and I felt strangely uneasy. Although Joe was talking to Graham, he was looking at me differently. Dare I say accusingly? He did not seem happy and I'm sure Graham thought everything was fine, but there was something that I just couldn't put my finger on, and it left me with a stomach like a churning sea and a growing feeling of unease.

I made my excuses and told Graham that I needed to have an early night. Ever the gentleman, he agreed without fuss, got up, hugged me and said that he would see me the following day. He shook Joe's hand and left. This time when the cold night air blew in as the door closed, it seemed to linger leaving a chill in the room.

Joe walked out of the room and up the stairs. He didn't look at me and didn't speak. I felt uneasy and confused and I tried to think of what I'd done wrong but my brain was fuddled with grief, lack of sleep and wine.

I hopped in the shower when Joe got out and tried to make conversation with him as I got into bed. He turned his back.

"Go to sleep, Charlotte. I'm tired as well."

"Oh, OK then. 'Night. I love you."

Silence! Nothing wrong in the words he'd said but I felt that there was a whole chapter of unsaid words between us. I slept terribly all night despite being exhausted. I couldn't stop thinking of how Joe had behaved and this was the first night since our wedding that he'd not kissed me goodnight and told me that he loved me. There was definitely something up.

I woke in the morning after drifting off to sleep at some point early morning. My eyes were puffy and sore and I felt like I'd been hit by a sledge hammer. A wave of nausea rose inside me and I ran to the bathroom and vomited.

I had just stepped out of the shower and into the bedroom when Joe came in.

"Morning, gorgeous. How you feeling?"

I wrapped my arms around him and snuggled into him, loving that I felt safe and secure and happy that he was back to the Joe that I knew and loved. I couldn't keep up with his moods, but it didn't matter because all I wanted was peace and no arguments.

"I feel a bit fragile but I didn't sleep well, and I've been sick." I said, not looking at him.

"That's because you were drinking. I don't think it's a good idea, you drinking in the house, especially if you're going to make yourself ill."

I was speechless for a moment and my brain was trying hard to come up with something constructive to say like, 'Both my parents have just fucking died and I've not slept properly for days,' or, 'It's my parents funeral today, what the fuck do you expect?' but before I could answer, Joe trotted down the stairs, shouting up as he went.

"Sausage, mushrooms and tomatoes for breakfast?"

It was more of a statement than a question.

I headed back into the bathroom and threw up again.

CHAPTER 6

Getting dressed for the funeral, I was shaking so hard that I had to take a diazepam to help steady me. It helped stop the tidal wave of anxiety that washed over me but the downside was it made me feel detached from reality, almost as if I was seeing and talking to people through a thick Perspex window. However, I favoured that today, rather than the nauseating, ice-cold adrenalin that pumped through my veins on a daily basis as of late.

My aunt Trish and uncle Tommy had arrived the day before. Thankfully Joe had told them that I was in bed, it hadn't been a lie, however I had been awake but I'd not been able to face the emotional frenzy that would ensue.

They turned up to the house an hour before the hearse was due to arrive to take us to the church. Aunt Trish collapsed and cried salty tears all over me while I stood, numb and detached from the enormity of the situation and the medication that I had taken earlier. She felt guilty because my parents had been on the way to visit them. I assured her she was in no way to blame but grief does awful things and no matter what I said, she remained firm that it was her fault.

I zoned out at the funeral and focused on the stained glass window and the back of the church. It emitted a rainbow of hazy light and highlighted dust motes that hung, suspended in the air. Occasionally they moved as a gust of wind squeezed through the windows and under the door. It was always windy here no matter what time of year it was.

I found it easier to look at the brightly coloured glass, held in place by thick lead strips, than listen to the maudlin hymns and reverence to God. I questioned if there was a god in my head, and if so, why *my* parents? Why now? They would never get to see grandchildren or see our very first house. My breath caught in my throat as the reality hit me, and my legs gave way as a heart-rending cry broke free. Joe caught me before I crashed to the floor and sat me down. My chest hurt and I felt as if my tongue was swollen to double the size. I waited until everyone had left the church and I felt a little calmer, and I made my way to the wake.

People had waited respectfully outside until I arrived. I wanted to thank them all but words were stuck in my throat and I felt as if I had lost the ability to speak, so instead I smiled weakly as I walked past. I only stayed for a short while and then I left. I went home and I broke down. Joe held me tightly as I cried myself to sleep.

The following morning I felt strangely empty. The funeral was over and I was relieved about that, but in a strange way that had taken up most of my head space, and now that it was over I felt suspended in time. I had a void as big as the Grand Canyon in my life and yet I was supposed to carry on as normal. I constantly thought about my parents, but sometimes I would forget that they were no longer alive. A fleeting thought would enter my head about calling around to their house, and then a fresh wave of shock and pain would hit me.

Aunt Trish and Uncle Tom called around to say goodbye. They were heading straight back to Scarborough because they had left the girls with a friend. They had thought them both too young to attend the funeral and I had agreed. Why put anyone through that unless absolutely necessary, I would have gladly backed out myself yesterday, if I'd had the option.

"If there's anything you need, anything at all, you call us, OK? Please, Charlotte. I will never forgive myself for pushing them to come and visit us. We're always here for you."

"Thank you, Aunt Trish, that means a lot. Please stop feeling guilty, because it wasn't your fault. Give my love to Scarlett and Helen."

I hugged her and kissed her on the cheek. I knew she meant well but to be honest, I found her too dramatic for my liking. She was always full of hysteria and drama and I remembered my mum saying that she'd been like that since she was a little girl. I waved them off, relived that I could mourn in peace without having to listen to other people tell me tales of *their* grief. My head and heart just didn't have the room for it.

****

I booked an appointment to see Dr. Walter for the following day and lay around in a daze until I was forced to leave the house.

I hated going to the doctor's - nosy people wondering why you're there, making small talk in the hope that they can find out some juicy gossip. I was pleased when my name was called after a few minutes and I escaped the stares to take a seat in the doctors room.

"How are you Charlotte? I know it is very early days but are you looking after yourself?"

"Joe is looking after me, Doctor, but I just feel so numb." I said, crying. "Sorry, I just can't help it. I feel exhausted yet I can't sleep and I feel sick. I am crying literally non-stop and I feel like I have no control over it. The emotion just sweeps over me and I start to sob uncontrollably."

"The early stages of grief are very unpleasant and the best thing you can do is rest and take care of yourself. I am writing you a sick note for two weeks, but if you need another one you come along and see me before this one runs out, OK? I will also give you a prescription for some more diazepam. It's a low dose so there's no need to worry and you just take one or two whenever you feel overwhelmed. They will help you sleep and allow your body time to heal and adjust to the shock."

I grabbed the prescription and sick note and headed back home, avoiding eye contact with people as I walked. Luckily the weather was windy and rainy so I pulled my hood half over my face, pretending that I was shielding myself from the weather: the reality was that I was shielding myself from people; people who knew my parents and reminded me of what I had lost.

I was almost home when the strangest thing happened. I saw my mother walking quickly on the other side of the road, fighting against the wind. She was wrestling an umbrella that had blown inside out and it looked like she was fighting a losing battle. I was just about to cross the road and shout out to her when she turned and I realized that it was Mrs Thompson. I ran the rest of the way home and slammed the door shut behind me. My heart was pumping at a rate that left me breathless and I felt a mixture of despair, confusion and guilt. I berated myself for being stupid enough to think she could be alive.

The next few days moved along in a strange silence, mixed with bursts of grief that left me drained and confused.

Jimmy and Graham waved goodbye and urged Joe and I to visit for a holiday. People passed by and knocked to ask how I was doing and let me know that they were there for me if I needed anything. The conversations were brief and awkward, the words hurriedly spoken, as if scalding the mouth of the person speaking them. It was a relief to make my excuses and close the door on them.

Joe was strong and supportive but he felt that I would be better at work. I was still feeling ill though and getting out of bed in the morning was getting harder and harder. However, I agreed to return to work after my sick note ran out, even though I felt terrified.

Nicki returned six days after my parents' funeral. She had been to visit her grandparents in Spain. She knocked on the door and when I opened it she almost knocked me off my feet.

"Lotti, oh God, I just found out." She started to sob. "I am so sorry, babe. I can't believe you've been through all of this on your own."

I wiped my eyes. "I wasn't on my own, Nik. I had Joe and he's been so good."

I sat down and started sobbing, the trauma and shock hitting in fresh waves. "Sorry, Nik. I just can't seem to pull myself together. I have to go back to work in just over one week and I'm not sure how I'm going to do it. Joe thinks too much time sitting around is making me worse."

"Wow that's harsh! Give yourself time to come to terms with it Lotti. You've just lost both of your parents. You need time babe."

"I know, but I do think Joe has a point. Sitting around the house thinking is not going to bring them back and it's just prolonging my agony. I need distraction."

"I understand, but don't let Joe push you into something you're not ready for. If you can't go to work, go to the doctor's and get another sick note.

"Listen do you fancy going to The Barn Owl in Warkworth for tea and a few drinks? My treat. I just think it would be good to get out of Alnmouth and away from everything that reminds you of your loss for a few hours. I'll drive us there and leave the car and we can get a taxi back."

"Yeah, OK. That sounds lovely. What time?"

"I'll pick you up at six."

Nicki grabbed me in a bear hug and kissed my cheek. "Never forget, Lotti. I'm always here, no matter what."

I spent the rest of the afternoon preparing Joe's tea and then I decided to spruce myself up.

I put a treatment on my hair and wrapped it in a towel while I painted my toenails. It felt good to be doing something girly and Nicki was the only one that could make me smile through a black cloud.

I texted Joe to tell him of my plans and was a little shocked at his reply. I asked if he minded if I went out for tea with Nicki and he replied, 'I guess it doesn't matter what I think as it seems you've already made your plans.'

He came in from work and was clearly not in a good mood. He went straight up for a shower and when he came down he turned the TV on and barely acknowledged me.

"I've made you chilli con carne for tea. It's in the fridge, all you have to do is heat it up. I won't be late in Joe. I should be back for ten."

"Already had something to eat. I wasn't sure you'd have time to see to me. Oh, and I hope this isn't going to be a regular thing. She's a bad influence on you and I don't think I like you hanging around with her. The trouble is she's jealous and can't accept that you're a married woman now."

I stood there, annoyed but nervous and unsure how to respond. I decided to say nothing in the hope that he would snap out of his mood. "I'm going upstairs to get ready," I said quietly. I could not fathom him out at times.

I put my plain black dress on and my black patent heels. Joe walked into the bedroom and then looked at me with disgust in his eyes. "You can get that dress off because you needn't think you're going out in that. It's called cock teasing and no wife of mine is acting like a single woman! I've already told you not to wear that dress unless you're with me, but you seem to go out of your way to upset me."

I racked my brain for a memory of the conversation about the dress and couldn't find one. Joe had walked over to me and was standing with his arms crossed, waiting.

"Joe, you have never told me that. I wouldn't go out of my way to upset you, you know that, but we've never talked about this dress."

"Yes, we have and you fucking well know it, so don't go acting all innocent with me. If you really can't remember, maybe you've just lost the fucking plot big time. I always thought you were slightly mad but you're getting worse." And then he pushed me hard enough so that I fell back onto the bed, and the imprint of his hand burnt my skin, leaving an invisible imprint on my heart.

I burst into tears and ran into the bathroom.

When I came out of the bathroom, Joe was downstairs and a pair of jeans and a t-shirt lay on the bed, next to flat black pumps.

I felt a mess. My excitement at going with Nicki was suddenly drowned out by this situation with Joe. I had puffy eyes and to keep the peace I dressed in the outfit that Joe had laid out for me and I headed downstairs, feeling nervous.

"Joe, will you speak to me, please. I hate this. I don't want to argue with you, especially after everything I've been through the past few weeks." I almost got down on my knees and begged him. My heart felt heavy with pain and my brain was working overtime, trying to figure out how to move forward. I felt wounded to the point that it physically hurt.

He looked at me, his mouth twisted, his eyes cold. "I've told you what I think and I don't think married women should be gallivanting with single friends."

"I'm not gallivanting, Joe. I'm going out for a meal with Nicki. She's just as devastated by my parents' death as I am and she's missed out on so much. We just wanted to get out of town and catch up."

The sound of a car horn penetrated the uncomfortable silence that hung in the air. "I'll see you later."

I leaned over to kiss him on the cheek but he turned away, then stomped into the kitchen and took out a beer from the fridge. He knocked it back, pouring the lager into his mouth as if he hadn't drank for months and then he let out a disgusting belch as he smirked.

I walked out quietly closing the door behind me and got into the car.

"How are you, babe?" Nicki asked as she kissed my cheek.

"God, don't ask. Joe has lost the plot. I don't know what's up with him." I had no sooner got the words out of my mouth when he texted me to say he was sorry, and that he had had a rough day at work. He told me to enjoy my evening and said that he loved me. I felt a huge sense of relief flood through my body and the knot in my stomach started to unwind, so I played the incident down as Nicki started questioning me about what had happened. She had a bad enough opinion of Joe. I certainly didn't want to make matters worse.

We walked into the pub, which was fairly quiet and ordered food, then sat next to the crackling open fire. "Lotti, how are you really? I mean it's such a shock and I keep thinking that it's all some big mistake. I can't imagine how you feel. You must be in pieces."

"I swing from being numb to being an emotional wreck at the drop of a hat, Nic. I am dreading the reading of the will in two days' time. I wish someone could go in place of me. The thought of sitting around discussing what's left of my parents' life just makes me shudder."

"I keep thinking of silly things like, they'll never see their grandchildren and it's heartbreaking. I forget that they aren't here anymore and expect them to knock on the door or ring me up. When I went to the doctor's the other day I could have sworn I saw my mum from the back. Do you know Claire Thompson? Well, she has the same coat as my mum and from the back I swear it looks her double. I honestly thought I was going to be sick. There just seems to be so many reminders everywhere."

I could feel tears building behind my eyes and I took some deep breaths to try and calm my overcharged emotions.

"I know, babe. I can't imagine how hard it must be. What do you plan on doing with the house, or have you not thought that far ahead?"

"I'm not sure. I guess we'll wait and see how the will reading goes and take things from there."

"Speaking of Joe, how is he? Has he changed his mind about having kids yet?"

"No. But I'm sure in time he will. Every couple eventually has children and I'm not in any hurry either. Plenty to do before we start thinking of that, but it will happen."

Food was brought to our table, and as appetizing as it looked I just wasn't hungry, and despite making an attempt to eat it, I ended up pushing most of it around the plate.

We moved into the bar area and had just sat down at a table after ordering more drinks when two men approached us.

"Evening, girls. Can we buy you a drink?"

I looked up to see two guys, one blonde and one dark haired. It was clear they were checking us out. Nicki started to smile at the blonde guy so I interrupted.

"Thanks but I'm a married woman and Nicki is taken, well she is for tonight anyway. Girly catch up," I said smiling in the hope that they would get the message and move on.

The dark haired guy looked me in the eye. "Married. Wow, you don't look old enough. Who's the lucky guy then?"

"I am," said a familiar voice and then all hell broke loose. Joe swung a punch and knocked the guy down, who then fell over our table, knocking drinks everywhere. The friend went for Joe, who ducked and then grabbed him around the throat. I sat back in stunned silence and Nicki was screaming and pulling at my arm, telling me to move. People came over to intervene and Joe was thrown out of the bar and grabbed me on his way.

"This is exactly why I didn't want you coming out tonight. If you'd listened to me none of this would have happened!" he yelled as he stormed off towards the car. He opened the door and virtually threw me in the passenger seat.

"Oh my god, you have to be kidding, Joe," Nicki screamed after him. "We were only out having a few drinks. Don't tell me now that Charlotte has a ring on her finger you're going to tie her to the kitchen sink. What you did in there was way out of order. We could have handled it, you selfish bastard. Charlotte has enough to deal with, without you going off like this."

"Fuck off, Nicki. Fuck off and leave us alone. Everything was great until you showed up."

He jumped in the driver's seat and before I could protest he floored the accelerator, turned the car and screeched away, causing me to bang my head against the side window.

"I saw you batting your fucking eyes at Tom Cruise. Jesus fucking Christ man, look what you've reduced me to! Following you around because you can't be fucking trusted to be near a man without throwing yourself at them and flirting!"

I turned to face him to tell him that it wasn't true and he slammed his foot on the brake suddenly, causing me to lurch forwards and bang my head off the dashboard. I screamed out in shock and pain and then I felt a hand around my throat, squeezing slowly at first and then harder, almost in slow motion. I'm not sure if it lasted seconds or minutes because I felt trapped in time, frozen in one single nanosecond that moved neither forwards, nor backwards.

Next second I was free. I gasped, gulping in air and sobbed erratically.

"Why did you do that? Why did you choke me?" I croaked and sobbed, and I knew that I sounded like a six year old child but the fragile bravery that I had built around me collapsed in a heap, leaving nothing but raw pain, panic and hysteria.

"What are you talking about?" he spat. "I didn't fucking choke you. You must have banged your head harder than you thought. If you'd worn your seat belt properly it wouldn't have happened. It's not my fault I had to stop for a dog on the road. And now I'm being accused of strangling you. Give me strength!"

My sobbing stopped as I tried to forge a connection between what I thought had happened and what Joe had just said. I could swear there had been no dog on the road, but maybe there was. I was almost certain that he'd put his hands around my neck but now I doubted myself. Maybe I had been knocked out and dreamt it. "What about Nicki?" I said suddenly. "We can't leave her there on her own, Joe. Please."

"Fuck Nicki. She's nothing but a bitch and she takes advantage of you, Char. You should choose your friends more carefully. Good job I'm here to look after you."

I cried quietly the rest of the way home. I felt so confused. Was it my fault or Nicki's fault? Maybe I had given those guys the wrong impression without meaning to? Why would Joe say something that was untrue? I was starting to think that he was right and I was going crazy. The thought terrified me.

I was worried about Nicki so I texted her and she replied, saying that her brother had picked her up and that she would speak to Joe about what had happened the following day.

When we arrived home, Joe was still ranting on about me egging the guys on. I told him not to be so stupid and he ran at me and grabbed my arm, before pushing me in the chest and knocking me off my feet. I landed awkwardly and felt a searing pain shoot from my wrist. I cried out in pain and he stopped. I thought I saw a fleeting glimpse of panic cross his eyes.

"What is it? Have you hurt yourself?"

"It's my wrist." I sobbed.

"See look what you made me do! For fuck's sake, Charlotte."

He seemed irritated and annoyed at me so I headed upstairs, out of his way.

A few minutes later he came upstairs with a bandage. He kissed me on the cheek and gently strapped my wrist. "See how it is in the morning. If it's still sore you can go to the doctor but maybe tell him that you tripped, because he won't think very highly of you if you tell him the real reason it happened. He's an old fashioned doctor and you're married now, as I have to keep reminding you. If he knows you were throwing yourself at another man … Well, anyway, least said about your behaviour the better. I forgive you. This time! You'll not be going out drinking with *her* again though, will you?"

And off he walked out of the room, whistling merrily to himself as I wrapped my arms around my middle and hugged myself as best as I could to try and take away the pain that sat like a permanent rock in my stomach.

The following day Joe was quiet as he left for work. He told me that we needed to talk that night so I spent most of the day feeling sick and wondering what he wanted to talk about. I was terrified that he would leave me, and although he had behaved badly the night before, I felt as if he was all I had left in the world. I now felt responsible for everything that had happened because I had played his words around and around in my head all day long and he was right, if only I stayed home, then none of this would have happened.

I headed to the hospital in the afternoon because my wrist was no better and I thought it might need X-rayed.

I was in agony and it was quite swollen so I thought it best to get it checked out.

I checked in at the counter and told them why I was there, leaving out the cause of the injury. I sat in the waiting area praying that no one I knew was in there. I was preferring anonymity more and more by the day.

A young nurse shouted my name and led me into a room.

"Hi, Charlotte, my name is Kelly. It says here that you've hurt your left wrist. Can I take a look at it?"

I held my arm out, wincing as she gently felt along the bone. "How did this happen, Charlotte?"

I felt myself flush slightly. "I fell down the stairs. I slipped on my dressing gown."

The words were out of my mouth before I had registered what I was saying. If I told her that Joe had done it she would judge me and I didn't want a lecture, so I thought it was easier to lie. "And these bruises? How did you get those?" she asked, pointing to my forehead.

I turned red as I relived the car incident of the previous evening.

"I - erm - I - do I - do I need an X-ray or can I go home?" I stuttered awkwardly.

She looked me in the eye for what seemed like an eternity. I felt as if she was telling me that she knew the truth. I suddenly felt hot and I could feel my breathing picking up pace. "Two minutes, Charlotte. I'll be straight back, just wait here."

Oh, God, what now, I thought. Was she going to call someone or bring another person in with her? She walked briskly back into the room and ushered me around the corner, pointing directions to the X-ray department. As I thanked her, she handed me a card. It was for a telephone helpline for abused women. I dropped it in the bin on my way to X-ray. I could just picture myself trying to explain that to Joe. No, thank you.

My wrist was not broken, just badly sprained, so I left the hospital with a bandage and some anti-inflammatory medication.

I texted Joe to tell him that I had been to the hospital to get my wrist checked out. He replied by saying that I had better not have been talking about our private life to anyone.

He came in from work with a huge bunch of flowers and a box of chocolates. He handed them to me then cupped my face in his hands and kissed me passionately and the next thing I knew he was carrying me upstairs where we made love. I felt as if I was living life on a roller coaster and I was struggling to keep up, but when I lay next to Joe I felt protected and safe. I was starting to worry about how he always seemed to gloss over his behaviour but whenever I tried to bring it up with him, he seemed to have the ability to twist words and incidents until I started to doubt myself. I wanted to talk about what had happened last night but I knew it would end in an argument, and I didn't feel strong enough for that at the minute.

"I guess we should get up and eat. I've worked up quite an appetite," he said as he kissed my forehead and smiled cheekily.

Joe made a grilled chicken salad while I lay in bed thinking about the will reading the next day. I went downstairs when the meal was ready and Joe had put the flowers in a vase and lit two candles. While we were eating he looked at me with a serious look on his face. "I've been thinking, babe, and I think it's best if Nicki doesn't come around here anymore. She's a bad influence on you and look at the trouble last night. If she hadn't pushed you to go out none of that would have happened. You're a married woman and Nicki forgets that. She's better off hanging out with single friends. She's trying to split us up. She's never liked me and I'm not letting her come between us."

His words were final and I knew it was pointless trying to reason with him. I sat there with what felt like a rock stuck in my throat. I couldn't speak and my mind was whirling with uncomfortable thoughts as I tried to make sense of what he was saying. Nicki trying to split us up? Nicki being responsible for the fight the night before?

I looked at Joe and started crying. I was just too confused by everything and wasn't sure if he was making sense or not. I was so sick of crying but I always felt so sad and anxious that the least bit thing started me off.

Joe hugged me and assured me everything would be fine. I decided to leave things for a few days in the hope that it would all settle down.

****

I had only been back to my parents' house once or twice since they died because it was far too painful. I could still smell Mum's perfume hanging in the air and Dad's waxy old Barbour jacket that hung in the doorway reminded me of beach walks and helping out at his allotment when I was younger. It just seemed to intensify the pain that I was already feeling.

Joe had been amazing and had called around on a daily basis to check that everything was fine. He had sorted through all of the paper work and had contacted everyone that needed contacting. I knew the next step was to decide what would happen to their house and the thought of it made my stomach turn as I sat outside the solicitor's office.

We sat in a very bare and basic waiting area that was clearly in need of an update and repaint. I hadn't had a lot of experience dealing with solicitors, but I always felt as if they worked in dusty old buildings. I could see the door from where we were sitting and the name, 'John Towart' stood out boldly in polished brass letters. He opened the door and greeted us with a firm handshake and showed us to a seat. This was the first time I had ever been in his office and it lived up to the image of what I thought it would look like. A solid teak desk framed with brass rivets and leather insert took up the main space. There was a grand leather chair, which John Towart sat in, and two comfortable chairs for guests. There were various files dotted around and a musty smell that seemed to penetrate everything, including John Towart. Dust motes seemed to hang suspended in all parts of the room, unmoving, as if the thick claustrophobic air was forcing them to remain still. I noticed the old sash windows were nailed shut and I desperately felt like forcing them open, and for a second I pictured myself smashing a window and sucking in cool fresh air.

Mr Towart cleared his throat, which forced me to look at him, and as I did I was aware that I was detached from reality. He offered his condolences and swept his chubby hand over the will that was laid out in front of him on his grand desk. His glasses were perched on the end of his nose and I noticed that he had bushy, wild eyebrows that stuck out in every direction. He had a kind face but had his practiced serious expression fixed firmly on his face.

He covered some basic information before the will was read out, and once he had indicated that he was ready, I tried to look out of the old rain stained window in the hope that it would make the process less painful.

John Towart cleared his throat again before he spoke.

"You, Charlotte Porter, are now sole owner of twenty two Corby Avenue and also beneficiary to the sum of eighty thousand pounds."

There was various references to odd pieces of jewellery but I didn't really take it all in. I felt as if I was having an out of body experience and was listening and looking at myself sitting there in the chair, numb and broken. I had no idea that my parents had that amount of money and I would gladly have swapped all of my worldly possessions to have them back with me.

I was asked to forward on bank details and then handed a copy of the will. I left the office in a zombie like state and headed back to the car. Joe had his arm around me and was also quiet. I think he was running out of things to say.

"You've had a tough day, babe. How about I get us a take out tonight and grab a bottle of wine and we can talk about where we go from here? Why don't you have a lie down when we get in?"

I couldn't even contemplate the thought of food, but nor could I be bothered to try and explain that to Joe because he would insist that I have to eat, so I nodded and went straight upstairs, closed the curtains and curled into the foetal position on my bed. There had been way too much information to take in and I felt drained. I closed my eyes and drifted off to sleep.

I dreamt that I was running through a field of lavender and my parents were walking with their back to me in the distance, holding hands. The smell was intoxicating and made me feel light-headed. I desperately wanted to catch up to my parents and I ran and ran, but no matter how fast I went the distance between us never changed. Eventually I collapsed in a heap and woke suddenly with my heart racing like a steam train and tears running down my face.

I could smell lavender and panicked, feeling confused.

"I've run you a bath, babe. It's four pm," Joe said as he walked into the room. "I was just about to wake you. You have a nice soak, I've put some drops of lavender in for you but I think I might have gone a bit crazy. It's supposed to help relax you, though, so it might help you a little. I'll go and get us some food once you're out and dressed."

Joe could be so sweet and thoughtful at times and a surge of love pumped through my veins and cleared my head for a few seconds before the blackness closed in around me again. He kissed me on the forehead and I forced my body to get off the bed. I felt as if I was weighed down with wet sand. My muscles ached and I felt unable to focus my thinking, and for the first time in my life I thought about drug addicts and I felt as if I understood their need to enter into a drug induced haze that was an escape from reality. Right now, I would welcome that.

I had little appetite as I sat looking at the plate of food. Joe was unsure what to buy so he bought three different meals. I silently cursed him as I looked at the dishes of lemon chicken, chow mein and curry. I swallowed the nausea down as I placed a small amount of lemon chicken, rice and chow mein on my plate. I put some food into my mouth and felt as if I was fighting against my own body and having to will my hand to move the food up to my mouth. It tasted of nothing and I was thankful for the cold glass of white wine to wash it down, because I felt as if my throat had gone on strike and was refusing to swallow. It was as if my inner body had died, leaving behind a shell devoid of any happiness or joy, even from the most simple of things like eating. The only thing I did seem to get pleasure from was drinking cold water, because it helped take away the choking sensation that grasped my throat on a daily basis.

"I was thinking, about your parents' house." Joe interrupted me from the cavernous depths of nothingness, a place I was starting to enjoy frequenting. "Do you want to rent the house out or do you think it would be best to sell it?"

I was a little taken back by the question and not sure I was even ready to think of that just yet, but I had to at some point, I figured. I tried to think about what I wanted to do as I pushed the food around my plate. "I'm not sure, Joe. We have money so there's no urgency for cash and I guess renting it provides some extra income for us. Still, I'm not sure I could stand the thought of someone else being in their house. It's too painful." "How about if we renovated it a little so it feels less like your parents' house? Do you think that would help? We could do one room at a time and sort through things as we go. Just take our time, baby, and it will give us something to do on the dark miserable winter days and nights on a weekend."

I smiled at Joe. He had really thought of everything. "That sounds like a good idea, although I have to admit I am dreading getting started, so you'll have to push me to do it, otherwise I'll just delay it as long as I possibly can."

"No time like the present! The longer you put it off the harder it will be, so we'll go tomorrow and we have all weekend. You can choose which room you want to start with and then we'll head to the DIY store for paint, paper or whatever we need."

****

As soon as I stepped out of bed the following morning, I felt a wave of nausea rise up from my stomach to my throat. I knew I had to go into the house today and clearly it was having an impact. I did wonder if now was the right time, but then again, when is there ever a right time to do such a daunting task?

I rushed to the bathroom and vomited. I felt sweat beads form on my brow and my eyes blurred as everything started to merge together. I sat on the floor welcoming the feeling of the cold tiles seeping through my pyjamas, reminding me that my body was still alive.

"You must have drank more wine than I thought, babe," Joe shouted through the door. "As long as you don't make a habit of it."

I couldn't be bothered to respond. I sat until the cold chilled my bones and then I took a deep breath and prepared myself for the job that lay ahead.

As soon as I entered the house, I expected to smell baking and hear the television. Instead it was eerily silent. Familiar smells still hung in the air and it felt as if time had been suspended and a lingering longing clung to me, making my heart lurch every now and then in the hope that there had been some kind of terrible mistake.

I had waves of crippling nausea and dizziness while moving furniture and sorting through personal items in the lounge. Photographs in albums were boxed and put to one side for a day in the future when I would feel strong enough to look at them. Some items I simply moved from one room to another, an avoidance technique that allowed me a bit of time.

We worked in total for four hours before I called it a day and admitted defeat. The stress was overwhelming and I felt exhausted. I felt no sense of accomplishment or relief at making a start on the house. If anything it made things feel more final.

I called Nicki when I got home and offloaded onto her. I had suggested that Joe go out the pub so that I could have some space. I chatted to Nicki for an hour before crashing out and dreaming of boxes. Boxes in every single room of my house. Boxes in my car and even stacked up on the street. Some boxes had arms and legs hanging out of them and I was unsure if they were dead people and I woke with a scream. It was pitch black and I put the light on and waited for Joe to get home. I was too frightened to close my eyes again and I was regretting starting on the house so soon.

Maybe tomorrow I would feel different, I thought, even though deep down I knew I wouldn't.

CHAPTER 7

I rubbed my arms as the cool night breeze clung to them. It always amazed me how quickly the body adjusts to temperatures. It was three am and I was sat on Cairns esplanade feeling the chill, even though it was almost twenty degrees. Back home in England that would be classed as a hot summer's day.

Margie still looked bright eyed and bushy tailed.

"Come on, don't stop now. I want to know what happened next. I want to know how you ended up here all alone in far north Queensland." She said.

I looked at her and had to admit that it had done me good to talk. The tension had eased and I felt lighter than I had done in years. There was no need to pretend anymore, no more blocking out those dreadful torturous memories, and most importantly no more living a lie. I had spent the past four years denying the reality and enormity of both of our actions: the past four years blocking out that day and the build-up to it. My mind, body and heart had been broken beyond repair and I had made sure that I would never be hurt like that again. Instead I had built a wall around myself, but now the tidal wave of emotions that I had locked away were threatening to burst through and eradicate any trace of that wall. It felt freeing to talk and that felt good. I had succeeded in my career, because all of my energy had gone into focusing on work, so that by the time I crashed into bed at night I had no energy left to think. After a while it becomes easy. The mind can be retrained to think and focus on whatever you want it to if you try hard enough. I am not a cold person or a harsh person in any way, shape or form but sometimes, life moulds you into a person that you do not want to be and the only way you can survive is to change yourself and reinvent who you are.

I looked at Margie, who was waiting expectantly.

"OK. I suppose I need to pick up where I left off so that you can get the flow of the story. You don't mind sitting here at three in the morning?"

"Not at all, darl. It's an interesting story and I'd like to know how it ended."

****

My first day back at work went as I had predicted. I walked through the door, I took one look around at the pained expressions from my colleagues as they struggled to think of something constructive to say, and I burst into tears. It worked in my favour though because it quickly cleared the air, and hugs and tissues replaced biting lips and avoidant eyes.

I settled back into work as best as I could, trying to keep busy, and I have to say that it did work to a degree. I felt less stressed than I had when I had sat at home thinking all day long, making myself ill. Some days were still a struggle but I got through as best as I could.

Things between Nicki and Joe had not improved any. I had arranged to cook a meal and I invited Nicki to the house. Joe knew nothing about it and I knew it was a risk, but I figured if I got them both together they would be able to sort things out.

I was wrong!

"Don't be mad, Joe, but I've asked Nicki around for a meal. I thought we could eat together and try and sort things out. I miss her and I hate that things are awkward between you two." I looked at him expectantly, but he just walked out of the room with a sneer on his face.

Joe stayed in, which was more than I had expected, but the night went from bad to worse. First Joe and Nicki argued about women's rights and he accused Nicki of being 'A fucking hairy legged feminist'. Then Nicki brought up our night out. They ended up having a huge argument and the atmosphere was electric with the potential to go off with a big bang at any minute.

"I'm sorry, Lotti, I can't sit around and listen to Joe's archaic views on the world. Text me or call and we'll meet for coffee, if he allows you to, that is!" and with that she stormed out of the house shouting, "Good luck, Charlotte," before slamming the door behind her.

And so that would set the precedent of Nicki and I meeting after work, or on a weekend when Joe was not around. We texted regularly but I hated that she couldn't call around after work and it seemed to change our relationship. We were not as close as we'd once been and things felt awkward between us.

****

Despite my initial reluctance, my parents' house was coming along nicely and we had decorated all but one of the bedrooms. I had spoken to a rental agency and had decided to lease the house through them, so that I had as little as possible to do with it all. I had set up a separate account that would act as a savings account for our retirement. This was Joe's idea and I thought that it was a great one. This account would give us a hefty nest egg, which I'm sure Joe had already half spent with his travel plans for the two of us.

Things between Joe and I were up and down and there were times when he would accuse me of things that I hadn't done. For example, if we went out for a night, which was rare, Joe would say that I was flirting with men or staring at them. I was sure that I didn't but he would get so upset about it that I started to doubt my sanity at times. We would end up having a row and then he would apologize the next day and tell me it was because he loved me so much and couldn't stand the thought of losing me.

Joe was unhappy at work and did not get along well with his boss. They'd had a disagreement but he wouldn't tell me what about, but the outcome was that he started drinking more on an evening, and especially at the weekend and as a result of this, his temper became worse. He would sometimes walk in from work and start ranting about his boss, Dave, telling me out loud what he would like to do to him. It scared me that he could be so cold when he was talking about 'smashing his face in'.

When Joe had been drinking he would become like Jekyll and Hyde. We could be laughing one minute and then the next he would be criticizing my weight loss.

"Look at the state of you, Charlotte," He'd say. "You're so fuckin' skinny and ugly. No one would ever look at you now. Just as well you're already taken or you'd end up on the shelf. I can't believe how much you've changed since we first met. You used to be attractive."

He would laugh after he'd said it and I would feel pain tear through my body and stop at my heart before it rippled through it. I couldn't believe that he would say those things to me and it destroyed me to think that he saw me that way.

I would look in the mirror and examine myself. I knew that I had lost weight since my parents' death and I probably was too thin, but I'd been through a lot.

It's strange what the mind absorbs; and when you are told something often enough you start to believe it. So it didn't take long before I started to see an ugly, skinny person staring back in the mirror.

****

One Thursday night Joe wanted to go out to the local because there was a charity darts night on. I was happy to stay in but I could see him getting agitated, so for the sake of peace I agreed to go along. I was always careful what I wore and checked with Joe that he was happy with the outfit. I wore jeans and a fitted top and heels. I barely wore make-up because Joe said it looked trashy on me. I dreaded these nights out because they had the potential to end in disaster, but if I refused to go, I was boring and I'd then get the threats of 'marrying to young' hanging over me.

We were having a good night. Joe was playing the odd game of pool with some of the locals and I stood at the bar, watching. The atmosphere was relaxed and for the first time since the death of my parents, I allowed myself to laugh and I started to relax a little and enjoy myself. I was standing at the bar at around ten pm when I felt a tap on my shoulder. I turned around.

"Charlotte. I thought it was you."

Shaun Phillips was standing in front of me smiling. I hadn't seen him since I had left school and he had joined the RAF. "Hey, how are you?" I asked, smiling.

Shaun stepped in and hugged me before I could stop him. "You're looking well," he said.

I felt confused and defensive and was not sure how to reply to that comment. Joe told me on many occasions that I looked terrible, too skinny and ugly, and yet here was someone I'd not seen for years telling me I looked well, and he seemed to be genuine.

"Who's this, then?" Joe's voice interrupted as he grabbed hold of my elbow a little too firmly, discreetly squeezing it tightly, causing me to flinch.

I felt my stomach churn and my hands start to shake. It was clear to Shaun that I was uncomfortable but Joe was friendly, shaking Shaun's hand, introducing himself and buying him a drink. I hadn't expected that and I started to relax and join in the conversation. We stayed until closing time and all in all, I felt as if we had had a really good night. We walked home with two other people who lived a few streets away and everything was fine until they left. Then the silence hit like a stone wall. I started feeling edgy but thought maybe I was over reacting.

I had no sooner shut the door behind me when I felt Joe's fist slam into my face, along with a string of words that seemed to hurt just as much as the fist.

The next thing I knew I was lying on the sofa and Joe was crying and wiping my forehead and face with a damp towel. He was rambling on about being sorry and then said it was my fault because I'd been coming on to Shaun. "Look what you've made me do, Char!"

He held his head in his hands and cried. It may sound crazy, but I actually felt sorry for him and I knew that he regretted it. He asked me how he was supposed to trust me when I behaved in such a way.

I couldn't speak. My mind was reeling backwards and I was thinking that I must have missed something because I couldn't actually remember doing anything other than talking.

My head was pounding and my eye was swollen to the point where I could barely open it. My cheekbone was throbbing and I felt sick. The emotional pain at what had just happened by far outweighed the throbbing pain of my injury. I wanted to curl up into a ball and cry myself to death. I felt overwhelmed by the reality of what Joe had done, and I decided there and then it was easier if I did not go out at all. I was so confused.

Maybe I did give men the wrong impression. I mean I must for him to do something this drastic.

"You don't understand how much I love you and you keep egging men on and then, well, look what has happened. I'm starting to think that we are a bad idea. You know I love you, but you make me do things and I think it's probably best if I leave."

I felt my heart stop and adrenalin course through my body and despite lying there, battered and bruised, I jumped up and begged him not to go. I couldn't stand the thought of losing him when he was the only thing that I felt I had left in my life. My heart felt as if it was breaking in two and the pain I felt was so intense I seriously wondered if I would die.

Joe walked out of the house, slamming the door behind him. I was a complete wreck. I didn't know what to do or where to go. I lay on the bathroom floor after vomiting and shuddered as the last sobs escaped from my body. I closed my eyes and for the umpteenth time I prayed that when I woke in the morning, everything would be fine.

A closing door at seven am woke me from my fragile state of sleep. I half sat up as I heard footsteps coming up the stairs. My head was spinning intermittently and I knew that my face was swollen where Joe had hit me. I could barely open my eye and wondered if there were any broken bones. I was too frightened to bring it up and too embarrassed to go to hospital in case I bumped into someone that I knew. I texted my boss to say that I would not be going into work.

Joe walked into the bathroom and crouched down next to me. He looked at me and I tried to work out what he was thinking. I waited for him to speak as my heart raced inside my chest, sending blood rushing to my ears like a distant beating drum. I never knew where I was with him lately and I was never sure of what his next move would be.

"I had to go. You understand that, don't you?" he said quietly, looking at the floor.

His calmness unnerved me and I found myself nodding, even though I disagreed with him and understood none of his actions. I had still had not fathomed out how I had thrown myself at Shaun: nor did I understand why Joe had hit me. As for him leaving, I was completely thrown by him walking out and now that he had done it once I feared that he would do it again. I felt as if I was in a waking, living nightmare that there was no escape from. All I wanted was for things to go back to how they used to be. I felt my body shaking with anxiety and fatigue as I waited breathlessly for Joe to say something that would reassure me that things would be OK.

He glanced at me and smiled, but it was not a smile that reached his eyes. His eyes were cold, and I felt adrenalin rush through my veins like ice, causing my heart to skip a beat and my lungs to shrink. I felt as if there was not enough oxygen going into my body and at that moment I became acutely aware that the very thing that was keeping me alive, also seemed to be slowly suffocating me.

"Look at the state of you. What a mess," he said gruffly. "Get a shower and we talk when I get in from work tonight, baby. There need to be some changes around here if our marriage is going to work."

My stomach lurched when he said that. What did he mean, *if* the marriage was going to work? A feeling of uncertainty settled inside of me like a familiar friend. Shakily I stepped into the shower. My head was pounding from a combination of being knocked unconscious and crying half the night. I decided that I would just put my pyjamas and dressing gown on. I had no intention of going anywhere today, apart from bed.

I was waiting for Joe when he came in from work at seven pm. He'd clearly gone straight to the pub when he'd left work because he finished at five.

I'd been thinking all day about where he had slept last night. I hadn't thought to ask him this morning even though it had played on my mind, but he'd been in and straight out to work, leaving me wondering about what he needed to talk about now.

The door slammed and he walked in confidently, smiling as he sat opposite me.

"I've done a lot of thinking, Char, and we can't go on like this. You're making me do things that I have no control over and I hate what's happening between us. I think what we need is a new start. I passed the estate agent on the way here and there's a house just come on the market on River Mews. It's a bit more expensive than I'd like, but you have the eighty thousand pounds from your parents, so we will have more than enough for a deposit. I thought we could go and view it tomorrow." He smiled excitedly, while he stared at me with his mesmerizing blue eyes, giving me a glimpse of the Joe that I knew and loved so very much.

I felt as if the breath had been knocked straight out of me! I'd gone from contemplating the future of my marriage to spending my inheritance in a blink of an eye. I wasn't sure I wanted to buy a house at the drop of a hat and although I intended to use my parents' money at some point I wasn't sure now was a good time. It had only been four months since they died. I was aware that if I put up any objections Joe would … Joe would … Well, I wasn't sure what Joe would do anymore. Whatever I did or didn't do seemed to upset or annoy him. I saw the way he looked at me sometimes and I'm sure there was loathing in his eyes but then he would make love to me and tell me I was his princess and I would believe that everything was OK.

"What about my face, Joe? I can hardly go wandering the streets with this cheek and eye. People will ask questions and talk." I said nervously.

"You'll tell them that you were drunk, fell down the stairs and bashed your face on the coat stand. I'm off to email the estate agent, get yourself dressed, you're like an old woman lying around in pyjamas at this time of day."

I wanted to object but I knew that we would be back to square one, so I decided to go along with it. After all, looking never did any harm and it wasn't as if we needed to make an offer.

The following morning I got dressed, despite my pounding head and swollen face and we drove the short distance to the house.

The agent was waiting for us as we pulled up.

"Take no notice of her face," Joe said, smiling as he stepped out of the car and shook her hand. "You've no idea what I have to put up with. She was that drunk last night that she fell from the top of the stairs to the bottom. Almost took me with her!" He raised his eyes in a way that insinuated that he was really pissed off at me.

I went bright red and opened my mouth to say something, but thought better of it. The fact that I went red must have quashed any niggling doubts that she had. She cleared her throat and half smiled at me awkwardly, before starting to rattle off her sales pitch.

I couldn't believe that Joe had said those things and more worryingly, he had said them very convincingly, without a hint of remorse or empathy towards me. My familiar friend, anxiety, wrapped its arms around my nervy body and started to slowly fill me with fear. I walked inside, tagging behind him, unable to make eye contact.

The house was stone built and overlooked the River Aln. It had three bedrooms, a double garage and patio doors in the living area that opened out onto a small paved patio out front, with the most stunning view I had ever seen. The trees on the opposite side of the river gently swayed in the breeze, the grass was a lush emerald green in the distance, and the sound of the river slowly trickling as it meandered along was so relaxing. There were large oak trees along the riverbank and a bridge further down the path. I pictured myself with children, gathering acorns in the autumn and spraying them gold to hang on the Christmas tree.

Inside the house there were beech polished wood floors that ran throughout the whole of the downstairs, except for the kitchen where there were mottled white stone floor tiles. The kitchen was roomy and had a built in double oven, with all appliances hidden behind the exterior of the wooden cupboard fronts. There was a breakfast bar and a small breakfast table. The kitchen was situated at the back of the house with a reception room just off to the left. The reception room had a window that looked out into the back yard area. There was an open fire and dining table that looked as if it had never been sat at and two grand leather chairs in the centre of the room, which faced a wall unit full of books. At the front of the house there was a huge lounge room with a large open fire and enormous stone fire surround. Again I pictured children and large knitted Christmas stockings hanging from the fire and a plate with a mince pie for Santa and a carrot for Rudolph. There was also a downstairs cloak-room and overall, the house was much bigger inside than it looked from the outside.

The upstairs had cream carpets and a big master bedroom with three pane bay window and a built in window seat. The views were spectacular. I could picture waking up and opening the curtains, being greeted with the sight of the tumbling river gently rolling along, and various birds wading in the shallows.

Large built in wardrobes covered the back wall and a fancy chandelier hung from the ceiling, catching the sunlight at different angles, sending off a mirage of dancing blue, purple and yellow silhouettes against the wall. The other two bedrooms were a good size and I imagined a nursery as soon as I walked into the room nearest the master suite. In my mind I could see a cot with drapes above it and a musical mobile hanging. In the corner I could picture myself, sat in the nursing chair, feet resting on the footstool, with an open window to listen the sound of the river as I rocked my baby to sleep.

The bathroom had a free-standing, old fashioned white bathtub with gold clawed feet. It was stunning. Everything about this house was faultless but I wasn't sure that it was me. It all felt a bit too grand.

Joe was off outside again, asking the agent questions. He certainly had her eating out of his hand. She laughed and giggled at whatever he said and occasionally flicked her false eyelashes my way with a look of disdain.

Joe walked into the back yard with the agent hot on his heels. I could make out odd words and I was positive that I heard Joe ask if he thought the owner would accept a lower offer.

"Well, what do you think, babe? It's amazing isn't it?"

I smiled and tried to think of an answer that would show my interest but leave room for a discussion.

"How about we talk about it tonight?" I said with more enthusiasm than I felt.

"As long as there's no wine involved." Joe laughed and winked at the agent.

I went red again. I hated myself for doing that because it made me look guilty. I walked off, got in the car and slammed the door shut. I could feel tears brimming, ready to spill over. I swallowed hard and closed my eyes forcing them back. That was something else that Joe had a go at me for. "Crying again," he'd say. "There's a shock! For fuck's sake pull yourself together."

He got in the car and looked at me.

"What's up with you stroppy?"

"How could you?" I hissed. "How could you fucking stand there and tell her that I was drunk and make a joke of what you've done?"

I felt sick as the words fell out of my mouth but I was so angry and upset.

"What would you rather I'd have said, Charlotte?" he spat angrily. "That my wife was throwing herself at another man and giving him the come on?"

"I did not give him the come on. I can't stand this. You're accusing me of things that I haven't done. It's driving me mad."

"Mm. Mad. There's a word that's been hanging in the air for a few months now," he sneered.

"What do you mean, Joe? I can't listen to your riddles today. My head hurts and I want to go to bed." "You've not been right since the death of your parents, Char. I've been wanting to talk to you about it for a while. You've lost it, babe. I think you should go back to the doctor because your behaviour is strange. You do things then deny doing them and try to blame me. I'm

111

not angry, babe. It's since your parents died. You do need to go to the doctor's for some tablets or something and you need to sort your shit out."

I sat stunned. I tried to speak but my mind was not capable of forming a coherent sentence.

Mad. Joe had said that I was mad and needed help. That I had lost the plot? Maybe I was mad, I thought to myself as he slipped the car into gear and pulled away. Was I imagining things? I didn't think I was mad but I must have something wrong with me, otherwise why would he say those things?

I went to bed for a few hours as I favoured oblivion over the living nightmare I seemed to be drowning in at the moment.

When I woke up Joe had made a casserole and set the table with candles.

"Come and have something to eat, baby. You need to start looking after yourself."

I smiled but inside I felt numb because I could not forget the words that he'd said. I decided that I would go and see Dr Walter on Monday.

We spent the night talking about the house and Joe was attentive and kissed my face where it was bruised. It was so confusing, never knowing how he would respond or if I was saying the right thing. I could feel the black cloud that was hanging over me, slowly growing in size and depth. Sometimes, not very often, a gust of wind would come along and blow the cloud away. Never for long though, as it would drift back and settle over me, smothering me, my perpetual nemesis.

Joe desperately wanted to buy the house but I was scared. It was two hundred thousand pounds. We had ninety thousand with my inheritance and savings but I still felt like it was too expensive. Joe worked out that we could easily afford the mortgage repayments on his wage alone if we got the mortgage over thirty years, and seeing as we were getting along well and planning for the future I broached the subject of children.

"Well, there is a room that would be perfect for a nursery," I said, smiling and snuggling up to him.

"I've told you before, Charlotte, I'm never having children so forget it. You're wasting your time. Anyway about the house. I think we should put an offer on it on Monday first thing."

"Joe, I'm not sure. It's such a lot of money."

"Baby, you have to trust me. I know what I'm doing. I'm doing this for our future. The house will be paid off by the time we are in our late forties and then the world is our oyster. We can go travelling and buy whatever we want. Can you not picture yourself waking up every morning and eating breakfast overlooking the river? On weekends I can make you breakfast and we can sit outside together listening to birds. I love the noise of the river. It'll be like being on holiday every day of the week."

It did sound tempting and it was obvious that Joe loved the house. A part of me wondered if a fresh start in our own home was what we both needed. It's not the best start to marriage, living in someone else's house. If Joe was happy then maybe we would get along and argue less and hopefully there would be no more repeats of last night, and so despite my initial doubts I went ahead and agreed that we would put an offer in on the house.

I made an appointment to see Dr. Walter on Monday morning and rang work to say I wouldn't be in. I felt bad taking more time off but my face was still a mess and I wasn't ready to answer questions from my work colleagues.

I felt nervous about speaking to the Dr. but as soon as I sat down in his room, it all poured out, along with a lot of tears. I left out the bit about Joe hitting me. I was simply too embarrassed and there was a part of me that blamed myself so I pretended that I'd tumbled down the stairs. I told him about the nausea and anxiety, and feeling exhausted and crying all the time. I wanted to talk to him about the accusations that Joe made against me but it was difficult to explain and I worried that it might make me sound crazy, so I decided against it.

Dr. Walter suggested that I take some anti-depressants for a few months, as the shock of the bereavement had most likely contributed to me feeling this way. He wanted to see me every four weeks to check how I was doing. So I left the surgery with a prescription for anti-depressants and a sick note for one week. I was devastated and a little bit embarrassed. I had hoped that there was nothing wrong with me but the doctor had confirmed my fears that Joe was right. I knew that I had bad days but surely that was to be expected after what I'd been through. I rang him to tell him how the appointment had gone, and he went quiet. I felt as if I had failed him and he did little to assure me otherwise.

He called me an hour later in a much brighter mood to tell me that an offer of one hundred and ninety thousand had been accepted on the house. There was no going back now!

Joe came home that night in a great mood. He talked non-stop about how great it would be to live in our dream home and how it would make going to work easier because he now had something to show for his money. His enthusiasm was infectious and I started to feel excited as well. Maybe he was right after all and this was just the new start we needed.

The following week Joe told me that he'd been thinking about changing banks because he wasn't happy with the service we were getting from our current bank. I wasn't aware of any problems but I listened as he talked about interest rates and mortgage offers etc. Joe had agreed that it was best if he looked into all of the finances seeing as I was 'not myself'. This phrase became the polite way of saying I had depression. On the not so polite days I was a crazy bitch who needed sectioned, or I needed to 'get off to the nut house where I belonged'.

Joe changed banks to a one outside of our village, which made it a chore if I needed to pop in for anything because I didn't drive. He decided that online banking would be the answer. Both of our wages went into our joint account and we also had our savings account, which was additional. We both had passwords so we could access the account anytime we wanted to.

It felt like just a few weeks later when we received our completion date. We had very little for the house with living in Joe's parents' house, but we had gift cards for Marks and Spencers and Debenhams from the wedding so we headed into the city to buy new things for the house. It was so exciting. We spent hours wandering the floors looking at furniture, bedding, and kitchen utensils etc. Joe was pretty easy going with furnishings but had an idea of what he wanted in the way of furniture. We ended up with a cream leather suite for the lounge room, which I didn't think was very practical, but as Joe reminded me again, we wouldn't be having children to mess everything up. We bought a small round cream and wood table for the kitchen, a new bed and some outdoor furniture. We decided to return the following week and buy everything else that we needed.

Eight weeks later we moved into our house and I had to admit it looked amazing, almost like a show home. The lounge was minimalist with just the leather suite, a sideboard filled with photographs and the TV. At night we lit a fire and the heat filled both the room and my heart, and I felt so proud that this was our house and I was sure that this was the fresh start that we both needed. Upstairs we had a solid wood bedframe with a huge ornate bedhead, which fitted in well with the large airy room. The bathroom was mostly white so I had bought some bright orange towels and placed some orange candles on the windowsill to add a splash of colour. Life felt good and the move had been a positive one as we were now getting along better than ever. Joe was attentive and showered me with love and on a Saturday morning, he would tell me to lie in bed while he made breakfast. Sometimes we ate it outside, depending on the weather, and other times I liked to sit on the window seat in our bedroom and watch the leaves fall from the trees and the birds flying from branch to branch.

My parents' house was all ready to go up for rent. It had been really hard for me to keep going back but slowly it had started to feel less like their home and more like an investment. I had been able to distance myself from it by making some changes. It had cost more than we had initially anticipated but we would make money back on it with the monthly rent. All of the wallpaper had been stripped and we had the walls plastered and then painted with neutral colours which made the house look a lot bigger, and we replaced carpets with laminate flooring and fitted new blinds at the windows. It finally felt as if things were starting to move forward and I was starting to feel positive for the future.

****

That weekend it was my birthday and I sat looking out of the window as I opened the present that Nicki had bought me. It was a solid silver heart necklace. We still exchanged gifts even though we did not see each other that often.

I decided to wear the necklace because Joe was taking me out to an Indian restaurant in Newcastle.

I was dressed in my red fitted dress and black heels. I knew I would freeze because it was October but it was worth it to feel nice for once. I had the necklace on that Nicki had bought me and I had bought myself a new pair of earrings. I curled my hair and then pinned it up and let a few ringlets fall loosely around my face.

"Wow, hello, sexy," Joe said as his hands wandered over my body. He held me at arm's length and looked at me before whistling. "You look hot, Char. You've put some weight on and your tits look amazing, just remember they're all mine. Give me twenty minutes for a shower and we'll be on our way."

We arrived at the restaurant just before seven o'clock. We sat in a booth, which was secluded and romantic with candles on the table. We ordered food and Joe pulled out a box and passed it across the table to me.

"Happy nineteenth birthday, babe." He leant over and kissed me. I couldn't believe that I was only nineteen because I felt as if I had been through so much already.

I tore off the paper and opened the box. Inside was a gold heart locket. I opened it up and a picture of my parents was displayed on one side, a picture of Joe on the other.

"It's beautiful, Joe. Thank you. I've never seen a locket like this before."

I look at him with tears misting my eyes. I could never fathom him out. He always surprised me when I least expected it. He really did have a good heart.

"You're welcome, gorgeous. Take that necklace off and put this one on. Where did you get that necklace anyway, it's new?"

"Nicki bought it for my birthday," I said nervously. "Oh well, never mind. You'll be wearing this all of the time to remind you of the people that love you. Now let's eat and get home so that I can rip that dress off you."

I flushed but felt an inner glow that things seemed to be back on track.

****

A few weeks later, Joe suggested that it would be a good idea to have a few of his friends around for drinks. I wasn't sure that it was a good idea. However, despite my hesitation, he went ahead and invited them around after their match that Sunday afternoon. I had cooked joints of beef and pork for them coming in, so they could eat hot beef or pork sandwiches. I did a huge dish of roast potatoes and placed a few nibbles around the house.

They all came in in a good mood after a three - two win. Joe had set up an old fridge belonging to his parents in the garage and it was full of cold beer. The boys put the football on the TV and some of them went into the garage for a game of darts. They chatted, laughed and swore a lot but they all seemed to be enjoying themselves. One of the lads called Karl headed over to me as I washed the empty bowls.

"How you doing, Charlotte? We never seem to see much of you these days. Have you become a recluse?" he asked quizzically.

It was a perfectly innocent question but I laughed nervously as I looked around the room for Joe. Sure enough, when I found him he was watching us. He gave a nod as if to reaffirm this.

I turned my back as I talked. I didn't laugh when I should have and I pretty much ignored Karl. He must have thought that Joe had married a boring, rude and ignorant woman but I simply couldn't go through another accusation filled night, or worse.

The music was loud and I could see that Joe was getting drunk and that worried me, so I quietly told him that I was going to bed.

He walked into the bedroom as I was getting undressed.

"Aw, sorry. Did you hope it was Karl?" he sneered in a loud voice.

My stomach dropped and I knew no matter what I said, Joe wouldn't listen or hear it. He grabbed me around the throat and started squeezing while whispering the words, "I saw you. You. Cock. Teasing. Slag. Do you think I'm stupid? Do you think turning your back so I couldn't see and hear the conversation makes it better do you?"

I clawed at his hand, trying to get him to let go of me. I could feel my heart hammering in my chest, and my lungs screaming in agony through lack of oxygen as blackness closed in around me. As quickly as he'd grabbed me, he let me go and I fell in a crumpled heap on the floor, gulping in mouthfuls of air and trying to focus my eyes that were still swimming out of vision. He gave me a hard kick in the leg as he left the room. I heard him not five minutes later, laughing loudly downstairs.

I crawled painfully into bed, and spent the whole night wondering what time he would come to bed and what would happen when he did.

I needn't have worried because Joe didn't come to bed at all. Apparently he went out to a nightclub in Alnwick and then to a friend's house until six thirty am. I didn't question him because a part of me was relieved that he had stayed away. The other part of me was broken hearted thinking about the possibilities of what he could have been up to.

Joe ate breakfast when he returned and then he made love to me. Actually no, no he didn't. Made love is the wrong phrase because that would involve passion, love and warmth. Joe had sex with me and it was aggressive and hurtful, almost as if he were wanting to punish me for something I had done - another part of our relationship that was changing for the worse. The strange thing is, when you love someone you don't always piece everything together to see a whole picture. Things are fractured and fragmented. You don't see things as they really are.

I had to take another few days off work because I had marks around my throat where Joe had grabbed me. He never apologized for what he had done and it felt too awkward for me to bring it up, so we carried on as if it had never happened. I felt as if I was spending my life walking on eggshells. Never sure of when the next blow-up would be or what would cause it.

A few weeks later I was told that there was going to be some pay-offs at work. The company had suffered some cutbacks and had recently lost a large contract, so we all waited to find out who would be amongst the unlucky ones and when it would happen.

I received my letter on Friday the twenty eighth of October, telling me that I had two weeks of employment left and that I would receive a small severance pay before officially becoming unemployed.

I told Joe nervously when I got home.

"Hardly surprising is it seeing as you're never there. I doubt they want somebody with a problem working for them," he spat angrily.

With that he walked out the house and I was in no doubt that he would be heading straight to the pub.

I wished more than ever that my parents were here for me to talk to.

CHAPTER 8

My last day at work was a sad one. The girls in the office bought me flowers and perfume and we headed out to a Greek restaurant for a meal straight after work. I was looking forward to having a few drinks with the meal and Joe had agreed to pick me up at eight o'clock. He seemed keen for me to go so I felt as if I could relax and it would only for a short while so hopefully he'd be fine.

I ordered kleftiko, an oven baked lamb dish cooked with garlic and lemon and served with potatoes. It smelt divine and tasted even better. We laughed and talked while we all ate and I felt myself relax as the wine flowed. Joanne, Kate and Emma had ordered a Greek meze which was a combination of small dishes, including meat, baba ganoush, olives, grilled vegetables, calamari, mini kebabs and hummus dips with warm pitta bread. There was so much food and for the first time in months I felt as if I really had an appetite, so I cleaned my plate and helped myself to some of the girls' food as well.

"It's good to see you relax and eat something, Charlotte. You're normally so stressy." Joanne said as she topped my wine glass up.

I smiled instead of giving a reply and felt tempted to tell her the real reason, instead I opted for more food.

We all chatted about jobs in the area and the conversation turned to what I might do next. "Stay in bed all day with that hunky man of yours, that's what I'd be doing," Emma laughed.

I returned the laugh and hoped that my face didn't give anything away. I felt flattered that everyone found Joe attractive, but I hated that no one knew what he was really like.

All too soon he pulled up outside and peeped the horn. "Tell him we'll get a taxi home, Charlotte, and we'll go to the pub for a drink. It is your last day after all," Kate said. "In fact, I'll go tell him,' Emma interrupted. She pushed her chair back and she was marching out of the door before I could stop her. "She's just going for a gawp," Kate said with a wink.

I sat, unsure whether to walk out to the car or wait for Emma to return. I tried to make conversation without looking noticeably uncomfortable as I waited for her to return. My stomach started churning and I was now wishing that I hadn't pigged out so much because I was feeling as if the food was going to make a re-appearance.

"All sorted. He didn't look impressed at first but he was fine when I left him. He said to enjoy yourself."

I smiled as Emma popped an olive in her mouth but I felt the knot in my stomach return. This was an awkward position to be in. If I stayed Joe wouldn't be happy and if I left to go home the girls would think I was rude and boring. I decided to go along to the pub but I would only stay for a few drinks and then leave. I texted Joe to tell him but he didn't reply. I rang him and asked him to pick me up at nine. All I got was, "I'll be there."

We drove home in silence and I tried to make small talk but I was nervous and Joe knew it.

"Oh, shut the fuck up. You're pissed and making an arse of yourself. And don't bother being all nice now that your friends have gone. You didn't give a shit earlier when you wanted to stay out."

"I'm sorry, Joe, it was awkward, Emma suggested -"

Joe banged the dashboard suddenly, causing me to jump. He pulled the car into the drive and slammed the door viciously after him. I walked in slowly hoping that he would calm down. I closed the door and nervously walked into the lounge. He walked in and headed straight for me and grabbed me by the hair, painfully pulling my head to one side. "Don't ever take the fuckin' piss out of me again, bitch. Do you hear me?"

He pushed me with so much force that I fell backwards, landing on the stone hearth. I scrambled away from the licking flames of the fire and forced myself onto my feet, and then I hobbled up the stairs and locked the bathroom door. I ran a bath and lay in it, numb from head to toe. I lay until the water turned cold and I shed a thousand tears in realization that this house had not made things better, it actually seemed as if things were worse. His violence was becoming more frequent and unprovoked. His words were becoming crueller and the lovemaking seemed to consist of sex on demand or rough sex that was not enjoyable.

****

I had looked for other jobs since losing mine, but either Joe didn't approve of them and said there were too many men in the office/workplace, or I didn't have the necessary experience. He told me to stop stressing and enjoy a few weeks off work. We had enough money living on his wage alone and there was someone renting my parents' house now, so there was no immediate pressure, but I wanted to get back to work soon because I wasn't used to having so much spare time on my hands.

Every morning before Joe left for work, he would tell me what he wanted for tea and set me a little challenge of cooking up new meals. Sometimes I didn't have a clue how to cook the meals he asked for and I had to google recipes online or go to the library. It was fun though and I enjoyed watching him eat what I'd lovingly prepared. "I could get used to this, mind, you being at home cooking me delicious food every day." He would say as he kissed me on the cheek. He was being really nice again and he seemed a lot happier, which meant that I was a lot happier.

One morning as I rolled out pastry, I decided that I needed some adult conversation so I texted Nicki to come around to the house on her lunch break. She worked in the local hair salon as a receptionist Monday to Friday. It had been a while since I had seen her. I had made excuses the past twice because I'd had bruises and even though Nicki was my best friend I couldn't bring myself to tell her how bad things really were. Besides, as Joe reminded me frequently, a lot of it was my fault in the first place. I felt as if I was going behind his back asking Nicki here, but I desperately wanted to show her where we lived.

She knocked on the door and when I opened it I was surprised at how emotional I felt.

"Wow look at me what a softy, crying. How've you been, Nick? I miss you so much and wish you could come around, but with Joe and everything. Well, you know how it is," I said awkwardly.

"I know, babe. It's difficult and me and Joe always end up arguing. Anyway let's not waste our time talking about our disagreements. I am desperate for a look around. Oh, my god, Lotti, look at this house. It's beyond awesome, in fact it's cool as fuck. I love it."
"Come outside and see the view from the patio and then I'll show you upstairs."

"Lead the way. Then we need a catch up because I've got loads to tell you."

We looked around the house and Nicki loved it just as much as I did. I confessed that I felt like a bit of a fraud living here as it was so grand. Nicki reminded me that the house had come at a high price and that my parents would want to see me living somewhere nice. "These views are amazing, hun. I would love to wake up somewhere like this every day. Speaking of such things, how's things with you and Joe? Or am I not allowed to ask?" Nicki questioned with raised eyebrows and a concerned look on her face.

I considered telling her the truth, but I was afraid that she would tell me to leave him and I loved him so much and despite everything, I really couldn't imagine my life without him, so I decided to say nothing.

"We're good," I said brightly as I glanced away from her, avoiding eye contact.

"I have some news for you, Lotti, but I'm not sure you'll like it," Nicki gushed and clasped her hands together.

"What kind of news? Tell me."

"I've been offered a job in Scotland and I've decided to take it. My current boss is opening a hairdressing salon in Edinburgh and she has offered me an apprenticeship plus a one bedroom flat above the shop. I'm leaving in ten days. I'm sorry, babe, it's just happened so quickly."

I was devastated. Even though I didn't see Nicki as much as I would have liked, I always knew that she was there if I needed her. We'd always been there for each other and now, well it felt as if my last remaining support was abandoning me.

"I'm so happy for you, babe, but I'm gutted that you're leaving. It's going to feel so strange not having you here," I said brightly, closing my eyes to keep tears at bay. I pretended that I was happy and excited but I felt hollow inside.

We spent the next ten minutes arranging a get together before she left. We agreed to go to a day spa to treat ourselves to some pampering and spend some time together, just the two of us.

Joe was furious when I told him.

"You've just lost your job and you're wasting money on things like that! Are you taking the fucking piss? Well, you enjoy yourself as I go back out to work so that I can keep you in this lifestyle!"

"It was you that wanted to live here Joe, not me! I told you I thought it was too expensive and I can't help it if I got paid off."

Joe walked off, slamming the door behind him and didn't speak to me for several days unless he absolutely had to.

The day came for us to go to the spa. I was determined to have a great time despite Joe's moodiness. And we did. We swam, had a massage, a pedicure, a facial and a manicure. We then enjoyed an afternoon tea of sandwiches, miniature cakes and cocktails in the large conservatory.

It was so hard saying goodbye to Nicki at the end of the evening, because I wasn't sure when I would see her again. She promised that she was only a ninety minute train journey away and said that she would be back at least once a month. We hugged and cried and promised to text each other every day. I returned home and Joe refused to talk to me. I went to bed after being accused of being a bitch and tossed and turned all night. I was grateful that I was not at work the next day because I knew that I would struggle to get out of bed in the morning.

The days ticked by and everything settled down and things between us seemed fine again. Joe's mood was a little off but I thought that maybe work was stressful so I tried to gauge how he was feeling so as not to annoy him.

The following day I went online to check the bank statement and had difficulty accessing the account. I rang the bank and they told me that as far as they knew there should not be a problem accessing the account so I waited until Joe got back from work.

"Hey, baby." I kissed him on the cheek and he pulled away slightly, causing my stomach to tighten and my mind to question why, but I tried to ignore my inner doubt. "I went online today to check the bank account but couldn't get on with my password. I rang the bank but they said it should be fine, so I'm not sure what's wrong. Maybe you should try and see if you can get on."
"It's all good. I changed the password."

"Oh. OK, well, can you give me the new password then, please?"

"Sorry, Char, no can do. You clearly have no value of money, wasting it on lavish spa treatments. You can't be trusted and what with you not working now, we need to watch every penny, so I'll be giving you a budget to do shopping etc., and you just make sure the money lasts, OK?"

I started to laugh because I thought that he was messing around, but he looked through me with his cold steely eyes and I realized that this was no joke. "You can't do that!" I yelled in disbelief.

Joe turned to look me straight in the eye. "Oh, I think you'll find I can!"

He walked up the stairs to get a shower and I sat at the table, wondering how he could justify doing that. There was nothing for it. I would have to get the bus to the bank and see if I could sort it out with them. Although how I was going to explain to them that my husband did not trust me with money and would not give me a password was a bit of an issue. I decided to sleep on it.

Everything was fine the following day so I decided to bring up the subject of money another time as I didn't want to spoil Joe's good mood.

****

That weekend we spent time planning Christmas.

Joe's parents were coming back for a few days so I suggested that we have them here for Christmas lunch. We would have our lunch and then light the fire in the lounge room and watch old movies. I planned on buying a real tree and I could picture the fire crackling, throwing out delicious heat, while the tree would twinkle and sparkle in the corner of the room and cinnamon candles would flicker on the mantelpiece, sending Christmas aromas through the room. I loved Christmas and everything that went with it. In particular I loved Christmas dinner with plump juicy turkey, pigs in blankets and cranberry sauce. My appetite had definitely picked up the past week or so and I was starting to fill out the clothes that had previously hung off me since my parents' death. However, the excitement of Christmas was also darkened by the constant reminder that my parents would not be a part of it this year. I swallowed back the memories and emotions and was determined to try and enjoy our first Christmas in our new home and make it special, despite how I felt. I had Joe to think of and he deserved to be spoiled and fussed over.

Joe was not at all keen for his parents to come here and he said that we would wait and see what happened. I wasn't really sure what we were waiting for but they were his parents and I barely knew them, so I left it up to him to sort out.

We ended up spending Christmas day on our own. It was actually really nice, considering how different it was to every other year. Joe made a special effort. On waking he told me to stay in bed. He went down to the kitchen and he brought me a tray up with a cooked breakfast, a cup of tea and a small glass of fresh orange juice. It was rather awkward trying to eat while sat in bed but I didn't want to spoil it after all of the effort he had gone to.

Once I had finished, Joe ran me a bath and told me to relax because he would prep all of the veg. We had cooked the turkey the night before so there wasn't a great lot left to do.

I came out of the bath and found a present on the bed. When I opened it up it was a black fitted dress that I had pointed out months back, when we were shopping for the house. I was touched that Joe had remembered and gone to the effort of buying it. I put it on, fixed my hair and walked downstairs.

"Wow you look amazing, baby. I knew that dress would suit you. It's missing something, I'm not sure what, but maybe Santa will have left you a little something to finish it off."

I kissed him and then led him over to his presents. He opened a new pair of football boots, which he had asked for and the rest he left until after we had ate. And eat we did. I felt as if I could lie on the sofa for at least three days without the need for more food. We watched Christmas movies with the fire crackling and it was almost perfect.

Overall, Joe was in a good spirits and he seemed happy with his gifts. He went into the garage and came back and handed me a beautifully wrapped box. Inside was an eternity ring, with seven small square diamonds set in it. It was stunning and I was completely blown away by how thoughtful and loving he had been. All doubts about him loving me vanished in that instant and I knew that everything would be fine.

We called around to Joe's parents' house on Boxing Day and had lunch. They made a traditional cold buffet of leftover turkey, salad, pickles, cheese and bread. We ate in silence and they attempted to make small talk but it was awkward and Joe was no better with them, so I was thankful when we left.

The New Year came and went, along with the icy wind and snow. I mostly stayed indoors during January, looking after the house and cooking. I quite liked it but I did get lonely and I missed working with other people my age. Jobs were scarce and the ones that I liked never seemed to impress Joe, so here I was, months later, still unemployed. We managed financially so I guess it wasn't a huge problem, but the days were starting to feel extremely long.

Joe wanted to go on holiday later in the year so we started looking at brochures. He fancied the Caribbean but I wanted to go to Ibiza. I was far from a party animal but I thought that it offered a bit of party life as well as a more laid back, relaxing holiday. We decided that we would book up within the next few weeks so that we had something to look forward to. Joe thought it might help me with the anniversary of my parents' death coming up.

The following morning I was due at Dr. Walters' to discuss the anti-depressant medication I was on, so I headed there thinking that if I didn't have these appointments to go to I would barely see anyone. Thankfully, I walked through the door as he called my name, so I avoided the dreaded time trap in the waiting area.

"Have a seat, Charlotte, and tell me how you're doing," Dr. Walter said as I entered his room. He always wore the same outfit of black trousers and the crispest, whitest shirts that I had ever seen.

"I'm OK, Dr. I am still quite tired but my appetite is starting to come back which I'm pleased about, because I had lost a lot of weight. I've not felt as tearful either, so maybe the tablets are starting to work. I'm still tired though and that gets me down a bit."

"Step on the scales, please, Charlotte and I'll check your weight, and then I'd like to take your blood pressure."

"I'd like to take some blood tests if that's OK with you, so that I can rule out any thyroid problems and I'd like to check if you're iron deficient. The results will take about three days and if you don't hear anything from me that means that everything is fine. I'll also take a urine sample to check how your kidneys are adjusting to the new medication."

I was busy typing out a job application two days later when the phone rang. "Hi, Charlotte speaking," I said as I juggled the telephone while trying to type.

"Hello, Charlotte. It's Hirst Point Doctor's Surgery. We have your blood results back and Dr. Walter wondered if you could call into the surgery at a quarter to five today?"

"Err, yes that's fine. Thank you." I said.

I could feel my heart rate increase slightly as my mind skimmed over the possible reasons for the call. Maybe it was low iron. I googled it and read some of the symptoms and decided that most of them applied to me. I relaxed because that could easily be treat with iron tablets or maybe even a change in diet.

As I entered the Dr's room and he ushered me to a seat, I was beginning to think that I should apply for a job, I was in the surgery that often!

"Thank you for coming in Charlotte. I have your tests results back and I think I know the reason for some of your symptoms." He paused and smiled at me kindly. "The tiredness and tearfulness and initial weight loss are all linked. Your results have shown that you are pregnant."

"Sorry," I stammered. "What did you say?"

I felt the blood drain from my face and the room seemed to shift in focus as I listened to the doctor repeat himself. Pregnant. I was pregnant. I felt sick, elated, petrified and shocked all at once. Oh, my god, Joe, I thought. How will I break this to him?

"We need to check how far on you are, Charlotte, so if you could just hop onto the bed and pull your top up so that I can have a feel of your stomach."

I lay on the bed and thought about that old saying, "For every death there's a life." A single tear trickled out of my eye as I thought of telling my parents that they were going to be grandparents and I felt a stabbing pain in my heart as I was reminded that I would never get that chance.

"Have you been trying for a baby, Charlotte?" Dr Walker asked.

"No. No, I - well, I know I'm married but I am on the contraceptive pill. I don't understand how I could be pregnant." I was aware that I was flustered and anxious.

"Have you been sick at all or missed any pills? Birth control pills should be taken at the same time every day, so if you have alternated times and then been sick as well, this could have been the time when you fell pregnant."

"I guess with my parents' death I probably have taken them at different times. I know I haven't missed any but I have been sick several times."

"Well that would explain the nausea and exhaustion. No wonder you've been feeling run down. How do you feel about the pregnancy?"

"I'm shocked if I'm honest. I really hadn't thought about children at this stage. I definitely want them, don't get me wrong, but I'm only just turned nineteen." I started to cry great heaving sobs and then it all came out about Joe's thoughts on children. "Joe doesn't want babies," I wailed. "He's told me so many times that he never wants children. I think he'll be really mad with me when I tell him."

Dr. Walter handed me a box of tissues. "You need time to adjust, Charlotte. It's a big shock but I'm sure once you tell Joe he'll be fine about it. Sometimes pregnancy can seem such a scary thing, but life has a way of throwing things at us and somehow we learn to adjust and cope." He smiled at me in a way that made me sad because I knew he didn't understand.

"He seems so against children and has told me that we are *never* having them," I stammered in between sniffles and sobs.

"Well, I would like to arrange a scan as early as possible so that we can see how far on this pregnancy is. It's difficult for me to judge and I don't want to get it wrong so best leave that to the experts. We also need to discuss the implications of the anti-depressant medication that you're currently on, as some research indicates that the baby can be at risk of premature birth and low birth weight. No immediate danger though at this stage, so don't worry, I'll give the hospital a call now and see when I can book you in."

I sat digging my fingernails into my hands as Dr. Walter spoke to the radiography department at the local hospital. I couldn't believe that I was pregnant. Part of me felt overjoyed and my mind raced ahead with pictures of a nursery and me taking the baby for walks along the river. Crisp white vests and cute bibs blowing on the washing line penetrated my mind and I got whisked along in a mini tornado of baby love. The other part of me felt terrified of Joe's reaction and the imminent changes to our relationship. I loved Joe so much but sometimes he was cruel and I lived in hope that he would change and go back to the Joe that I had fallen in love with. Every now and then I saw a glimpse of that person but sadly, he never seemed to hang around for long. I was now stuck, isolated and unable to leave for a number of reasons. I needed Joe, way more than he needed me, and I had no one else, it was just the two of us.

Dr. Walter broke my thoughts with talk of an appointment at the hospital for one week's time.

I left the surgery agreeing to return once I had been for the scan. We had agreed that we would discuss the anti-depressants at this appointment also.

I walked down the street in a daze, unable to believe that a baby was growing inside of me. Suddenly I became aware of prams and toddlers and cars with signs hanging in the back window saying, 'Baby on board'. The bus stop even had a nappy advert splashed across the side panel. It was if a baby switch had been turned on and things that I had never noticed before jumped out at me.

When I arrived home Joe was already in the house.

"Where have you been, Char? I was getting worried when you didn't reply to my text messages. You know I like you to reply within fifteen minutes so that I know everything is OK."

I looked at him and I felt my stomach do a somersault. I also felt an urge to put my hands on it in a protective way but thought better of it until I'd broke the news. I didn't know how to tell him and quite frankly, the thought made me feel quite ill. I tried to calm myself and tell myself that once he got used to the idea he would be fine. "I've been to the doctor's, Joe. There's something we need to talk about but I'd rather sit down and I need you to just listen, OK, and not react straight away. Please just listen because it's a lot to take in."

He followed me over to the sofa looking perplexed. "What is it babe? You're OK aren't you?" He asked as he grabbed hold of me and pulled me to him. I snuggled into his warmth and felt myself melt into his body. I felt a sudden rush of confidence that everything would be fine.

'I'm sort of OK Joe." I said nervously. 'The thing is, I'm not sure how you're going to feel about this and I've just found out, and it was a huge shock for me as well, in fact I'm still." "Charlotte what is it for fucks sake? You're scaring me, just spit it out!" He said loudly. "I'm pregnant." I blurt out avoiding eye contact with him. I could feel my heart hammering as I waited for a response.

He sat in stunned silence for what felt like an hour, but in reality it was only minutes. I glanced a look at him and he had turned so pale, he almost looked translucent. "How?" he asked in a breathless whisper.

"What do you mean, how, Joe?" I responded tensely. "You know how, but I think I must have taken my contraceptive pill at different times and then when I've been sick, well, well, here we are," I mumbled.

He sat stock still for a few seconds before jumping up, causing me to flinch in fright. "So basically you've fucked up and now you think you're gonna fuck both of our lives up? Is that it, Charlotte? Well I'm telling you now, you can get rid of it, and I'm not joking either. Have a termination because I don't fucking want it. You know how I feel. I've always been clear about that so don't start fucking around. Do what you have to but sort your mess out, and the sooner the better." He spat his words at me like darts, each one painfully stabbing me, causing pain. The thing with darts is that you can pull them out and the pain subsides. Sadly, that's not always the case with words. He walked outside onto the patio, slamming the door behind him, causing smoke to burst from the fire and swirl around the lounge room.

I busied myself in the kitchen for a while before returning to the lounge. I could see Joe sitting in the dark, the luminous moonlight outlining his silhouette. I walked away and went upstairs. I decided to leave him to think about it, after all I was still reeling in shock myself so it was hardly surprising that he was struggling to come to terms with it.

He didn't come to bed that night and I didn't sleep, despite being exhausted. Twice I had walked into the spare room next to ours, the one that I had already pictured as a nursery in my head. I could see a pine cot standing against the wall with white drapes hanging above at one end. I could see drawers with a wicker basket full of toiletries and murals painted on the wall and a closet full of tiny, adorable baby clothes - I only wished I could picture Joe in that room.

The following morning I got up to make Joe's breakfast while he was still sleeping in the spare room at the back of the house. I sat outside on the patio with a cup of hot chocolate and I imagined my life with a baby. Part of me did not feel ready for it but another part thought that it was meant to be. I felt so confused, but decided to wait and see what the scan revealed. I was a little worried because I'd not known I was pregnant, so I hadn't been looking after myself too well.

I came indoors and heard Joe moving around upstairs so I put his bacon on and made him a hot cup of filter coffee. He ate and drank in silence and chose to ignore me when I spoke to him.

Just before he left for work he turned to me.

"Are you going to the doctor's today?"

"No, I go to the hospital for a scan next week," I replied. I was hoping that after sleeping on it he would have softened a little. It seemed not.

"Why do you want a scan when you're getting rid of it?" he asked nastily.

"Joe, stop, please," I cried. "You can't just make my mind up for me. I need to know how far on I am and then we will talk about it. It's a huge decision either way."

"There's nothing to talk about," he shouted, and with that he slammed the door and drove off to work.

I spent the day in a strange void, my mind racing away with itself one minute and getting excited at the prospect of being a mum, and then the next, I would feel detached from reality and I'd be asking myself if this was really happening. I kept thinking of my mum and dad and I missed them more than ever. I cried because I knew if they had been here they would know what to say and do. I didn't understand Joe's objection: we were married, we had a lovely house and yet he would not budge on having children. Maybe if I could persuade him to go with me for the scan he would change his mind. It was worth a try, and I decided texting him was far easier than doing it face to face.

His reply was a very speedy, "Fuck off."

It looked like I was going for the scan alone.

CHAPTER 9

I had desperately wanted to tell Nicki about the pregnancy, but when I had rang her she was so full of excitement about her new job that it didn't seem like the right time. I decided that I would tell her in three weeks when she came to visit.

I walked into the hospital the next morning feeling nervous, and I prayed that I wouldn't have to wait too long before my name was called. I looked around the waiting room, as I waited on a scan that may or may not decide my fate for me.

I glanced around at the varying sizes of swollen stomachs. Some women who were clearly in the early stages of pregnancy sat around looking excited but apprehensive. The women who were heavily pregnant looked tired yet protective of the life growing inside of them, as they sat with a hand unconsciously massaging small circles on their expanding bumps.

My emotions were all over the place and I still wasn't sure how I was feeling about the whole pregnancy thing. Joe was determined that I would have a termination. Not one ounce of me wanted that, but I felt terrified of life alone with a baby. He assured me that our marriage would be over if I continued with this pregnancy, and part of me wanted to second guess him and have the baby in the hope that he would change his mind, but then another part of me: well, the other part of me thought about everything that I had already lost. The thought of potentially losing Joe on top of my parents was too much to bear.

I wasn't sure what I hoped would change with this scan, but at least I would know how many weeks pregnant I was and I'd have a chance to make a decision around whether to keep the baby or not. This was the complete opposite of what I'd dreamt about, in fact it was so far removed from what I wanted that it felt like some kind of sick joke or punishment. But the reality was, I didn't have support from my parents because they were no longer here; Joe's parents weren't in the area and he didn't have a close relationship with them anyway; and I did not feel strong enough to do it alone.

My name was called and I was led into a small room where a woman, who looked to be in her late twenties, introduced herself as Maddie. She asked me to lie on the bed then she placed a cold gel on my stomach, followed by a roller-like device. I felt unbelievably nervous and my bladder felt fit to burst. It seemed a lifetime before she spoke.

"Is everything OK?" I asked in a small voice.

I was trying not to get too attached to this baby in case I, well in case I couldn't keep it; and I'd promised myself that I wouldn't look at the screen, yet I could feel myself drawn to it.

At first I couldn't make anything out apart from a black and grey fuzzy image. The sonographer smiled and started talking as she pointed out the heartbeat and then traced her finger around the image of my baby. She started taking measurements and asked me if I had any idea how many weeks pregnant I was. "I'm not sure, to be honest, but maybe about seven weeks." I whispered, as a surge of love rendered me speechless.

"Well, according to this scan, Charlotte, you're eleven weeks and four days pregnant." She said as she smiled.

I let out a sigh of relief.

"Does everything look OK to you? It's just I didn't know that I was pregnant and I'm worried. I've drunk alcohol and not looked after myself very well. Does the baby look normal?"

"Obviously I can't guarantee that everything is one hundred percent at this early stage, but as long as you haven't over-indulged on a regular basis, I'd say the chances are the baby will be OK. The scan looks perfectly normal for a foetus of eleven weeks. You will have an AFP blood test done at sixteen weeks, which will check for any abnormalities, and the twenty-week scan can indicate the sex of the baby. So far though, everything looks good and there is a strong heartbeat. I'll email your doctor and let him know the estimated date, which according to my calculations, is the second of August."

I left the hospital clutching a copy of the scan and what felt like the weight of the world on my shoulders. How quickly life can change, I thought to myself. Eleven weeks pregnant.

I googled as much information about pregnancy stages as I could. I also checked at what stage of a pregnancy it was best to have a termination, and I spent two hours reading comments on a website from people who had been through a termination, and apart from a few people, most of them seemed to regret it, and go on to have another baby soon after.

Joe walked in the house at five pm and I put his dinner down in front of him.

I could feel an atmosphere and neither of us spoke at first. It was almost as if he was too afraid to ask and I was too afraid to talk about what the day had revealed. "I've been to the hospital and had the scan," I said as I sat myself opposite him at the table, unable to stand the avoidance any longer.

"And did you tell the doctor that you wanted an abortion?" he asked, as he stared at me accusingly, making me feel nervous.

"No, Joe, I didn't. I didn't see the doctor today, I saw the sonographer, the person who does the scan. The baby is due in August. I'm eleven weeks pregnant." I pushed the scan picture towards him.

Joe picked his dinner plate up and threw it across the room, causing it to smash against the wall, sending food and pottery everywhere. I stood to get up off the chair as he raced around the table to get to me. He grabbed me around the neck and squeezed as he spat out, word by word: "I. Do. Not. Want. A. Fucking. Baby. There is no fucking baby, so stop talking about it!"

He then threw me to the ground and walked out of the house. My instinct was to cover my stomach as he threw me down and protect the child that was growing inside of me. Instead, I curled into the foetal position and sobbed as I lay there detached from reality. I felt as if I was floating, my mind detached from the horror that had become my life. I ran a hot bath and lay in it, looking at my stomach and I wondered if the baby could hear the words that had come out of Joe's mouth. I wondered what the hell I was going to do. I went to bed and tried to sleep. Joe did not come home that night, nor did he reply to my text messages or answer his phone.

The following morning he waltzed in and walked upstairs to get his clothes for work. "Where have you been? I've been worried sick. You can't do this to me, Joe," I sobbed with a mixture of relief, pain and frustration.

"I can't do this to you!" he yelled accusingly before repeating himself. "I can't do this to you! You're the one that went and got yourself pregnant and for all I know it might not even be mine, and you have the nerve to complain about me!"

I stood there with my mouth wide open. What did he mean, it might not be his baby? "Why would you say such a thing? I have never slept with anyone other than you, and you know that. Please just stop this and help me. Stop pushing me away. I love you but I'm scared and I don't know what to do, and you're punishing me for something that is both our responsibility."

"I need time to think, Charlotte, but you can stop with the fucking guilt tripping, OK? It's always about you, Char. Every fucking thing is about you."

And with that he headed into the bathroom to get dressed, then walked out to work without another word. All day I played his words around in my head. I asked myself if I was needy and selfish. I didn't think that I was but maybe all the stress of losing my parents had damaged our relationship. I had been depressed and still was to a degree, but I still made an effort to cook his favourite meals and spend time with him, but obviously he felt that it wasn't enough.

I decided to listen to what Joe wanted, as it was clear that I had neglected him and our relationship. This pregnancy was clearly pushing him over the edge and while I'd felt confident and in control yesterday, I was now back to feeling vulnerable and helpless.

****

Joe came in from work late that evening after having gone straight to the pub for a drink. This was not a good sign. "So I've thought of nothing else all day apart from this fuck up," he said. He had looked at my stomach while saying the words 'fuck up'. His words were slurred and his eyes had a slightly wild look about them. "What have you decided? I really don't want this to come between us, Joe, and it doesn't have to. I love you more than anything in the world and I don't want to lose you, but you have to understand how hard this is for me. The baby might bring us closer together. We love each other, we have a house and a lot more than some people," I said desperately, hoping I could appeal to his softer side.

He came over and sat next to me and held my hand. It was the first time that he had shown me any affection since I had told him that I was pregnant. "I don't want it to come between us either, babe, but the reality is, it already has. I've thought about nothing else and I've tried to imagine us with a baby, I really have. I've made a decision and there's only one option, as far as I can see, if you want our marriage to work. It's non-negotiable though. You do as I ask and everything will be fine and we'll get through it. It might be hard but we will manage."

The words, 'It might be hard but we'll get through it,' stuck in my head. Relief flooded through my body and I felt myself relax. I knew deep down that he would see sense. I knew that things would work out. He had been in shock when I had broken the news to him. I was aware that Joe was talking as my mind was absorbing the fact that I was going to be a mum. "Are you listening to me, Charlotte?"

I turned to face him smiling. "Sorry, I keep daydreaming. It must be my hormones," I laughed.

"I want you to go ahead and have an abortion. Don't mention anything more to me about this, just sort it with the doctor and once it's done, we'll go on holiday."

I started to laugh, a hysterical, manic laugh that I had no control over. I could feel it bubbling up from the tip of my toes like a volcano erupting violently. "Are you listening to what I'm telling you, Charlotte? What the fuck, are you laughing at?" He asked with a look of alarm.

I walked out of the house onto the patio and let myself out of the gate at the bottom of the garden. Joe was shouting after me but I felt as if his words were wrapped up in cotton wool, muffled and distant, despite him standing at the door. My brain was fit to burst and I thought that I would collapse at any minute due to shortage of breath. My heart was frantically beating, like a hummingbird's wing in my chest, and my lungs felt as if they had stopped working and were no longer able to take in any oxygen at all. Despite this I walked until I could cross the bridge into the woods, and I kept walking until I found a large oak tree. I sat down and propped myself against it. It was cold and dark and I didn't care. I hadn't taken a coat with me but I wanted to feel the cold, I wanted to feel numb so that it would take the pain away. I could just see through the trees to the riverbank and random beams of light penetrated wherever a street light stood. The ground felt frozen and I wished that I could take something to kill the pain and calm my body. My stomach felt as if was doing flips and I thought about the baby growing inside me, oblivious to what was going on in the cruel outside world. "You're better off in there," I said out loud, touching my stomach.

It was clear that I had a choice to make - my marriage or a baby. Did I want a baby? Definitely. Did I want to raise a baby as a single mother? No, I did not. I thought about me pushing a pram and passing Joe on the street in the arms of another woman and I felt physically sick. I started crying and cried until I had no tears left and I could stand the cold no more.

I walked in the house and straight past Joe. He tried to grab at me but for once I brushed him off and stormed past him. He stood staring after me, obviously shocked at my despondent reaction. That night I slept in the spare bedroom. I lay awake until four am thinking, and then I drifted off to sleep. When I woke up it was ten am. I had a shower and headed downstairs. Joe wasn't in but there were two holiday brochures on the table and a note attached. 'Thought we could go on holiday afterwards. It would do us both good. Have a look and see if there's anywhere you fancy.' What a heartless bastard, I thought. I felt like taking a knife to the stupid brochures and slashing them.

I pushed a piece of toast around a plate as I thought about the huge decision that I had to make. It felt no easier in the light of a new day and any hope of Joe softening had been obliterated with his persistence about a holiday.

I decided that I was having the baby despite his reluctance. It made me feel sick to think of telling him and the possible impact it might have on us, but I simply could not have a termination. I had played it around in my head all night and I wanted the baby, there was no logical reason why we couldn't. We had a beautiful house, enough money to manage, and we were married.

I texted Joe to tell him my decision because I couldn't face another argument and quite honestly, I wasn't sure what his reaction would be face to face. I wasn't even sure if he would come home or not and a small part of me hoped that he wouldn't so that I could have some time to get my head around the whole thing. I knew that even if he decided to stick around, he wouldn't be supportive and I needed to prepare myself for that.

The atmosphere was tense when he walked into the house after work. He refused to talk to me other than to say he would be 'packing his fucking bags' at some point. I let him rant and said nothing because I knew it would provoke him. All I could hope was that with time he would get used to the idea.

Things were strained between us over the next week with Joe sleeping in a separate room and taking mysterious phone calls on his mobile. He was texting non-stop and he kept disappearing out of the house. I was starting to think that he was seeing someone else. He refused to talk to me or reply to any messages that I sent him. To say it was torture was an understatement. It all came to a head on the Saturday evening. He had been out during the afternoon, watching the football with a few friends and he was drunk when he came in. He asked me to go out that night and I said that I'd rather stay in because I didn't feel well, and I couldn't drink anyway.

That was all it took. He started ranting away to himself as he got another beer out of the fridge. He was shouting through from the garage that this was exactly why he didn't want kids, because the brat wasn't even here yet and already it was ruling our life. He threw darts noisily while yelling his pearls of wisdom through to the lounge and our surrounding neighbours. I was on edge and felt a building sense of dread but I was unsure whether to stay put and say nothing, or go upstairs out of his way. I decided to stay where I was. I was so sick of his moods and sick of walking on eggshells around him, trying to keep him happy.

I turned the volume on the TV up so I couldn't hear his ranting, and within seconds I heard him marching through to the lounge.

"Turn that fucker down. Now!" he bellowed. "Who the fuck do you think you are, Charlotte? You've fucked up our life and you -"

"Oh, shut the fuck up!" I yelled back, surprising myself. My head was about to explode and I felt all of the hurt, anger and anxiety that had been bottled up for months start to spill out. "I am sick to fucking death of hearing how everything is my fault. I am sick to fucking death of walking on eggshells around you, you stupid bastard. I've never met anyone so selfish in all of my life. Your mood swings, your drinking, your jealousy. It's all too much, Joe, and I've had enough."

It would be the one and only time that I would stand up for myself.

Joe flew at me and I felt his fist slam into my face, knocking me off my feet. I was aware that I had curled into a ball and I was trying to protect my stomach as the blows rained down on me, feet and fists pummelling without remorse - and then I felt an intense pain as blackness closed in around me like a weighted blanket.

****

I came to in a room that smelt of antiseptic. My eyes were closed and felt heavy. I could feel something in my throat clogging my airway and I attempted to lift my arm, but it too felt heavy, and weighed down. I managed with the other arm and felt something over my mouth, which caused me to panic. I forced my eyes open and everything was hazy and blurred and I could only make outlines of shapes out. I tried to talk but nothing came out, no noise, nothing, and I wondered if I was dead or having one of those nightmares that felt real, but then you wake up and sigh with relief when you realize that it was just a dream.

I heard a beeping sound and a door open and then a soothing voice spoke to me.

'Hi, Charlotte, My name is Lucy and I am a nurse on the intensive care unit at Wansbeck Hospital. Just relax love, you've been unconscious for four days. You have a ventilator in because we had to sedate you to allow your body some recovery time. I will try to wean you off the ventilator once you have fully regained consciousness. You're in the best place, sweetheart.'

I tried forcing my eyes to stay open but they were too heavy. I couldn't think of why I was in a hospital, but I was aching all over and my chest hurt. I heard the nurse's voice fade into the background as I drifted back into darkness. I was aware of background noise in amongst the black fog of unconsciousness, but my body remained limp and unresponsive.

I woke the following day and I still had no idea why I was in hospital. I tried to remember but felt as if my brain had been replaced by cotton candy.

"Good morning Charlotte." A small, dark haired nurse said as she smiled and stood over me. "Don't try to talk, lovie. We will attempt to remove the endotracheal tube in a few minutes. It shouldn't hurt but you may cough while I'm removing it. If you feel any breathlessness you must let me know as soon as possible. Just squeeze my hand because your voice might be a little hoarse and you might not be able to

157

speak up straight away. Is that OK? Are you ready for me to do this? Just nod or shake your head."

I nodded and although I had understood her, I also felt spaced out, confused. The next thing I was aware of was a pulling sensation in my chest and then I could breathe. My throat was sore and my chest felt heavy, and despite all of the sleep I had had over the past few days, I still felt exhausted. "How does it feel to be breathing unaided, Charlotte? Does it feel comfortable?"

I nodded, despite feeling like I had been hit with a truck. I tried to talk to her but a low whisper was all I could manage. "Why am I here?"

"Oh, lovie, you were brought in by ambulance. Do you remember anything at all?"

My mind travelled back to that late Saturday afternoon and an image of Joe in the garage, throwing darts and yelling through to me swam in front of me; as well as a recollection of me yelling, and Joe swinging his fists. I flinched at the clarity of the memory and the nurse took my hand in hers. "Are you OK, Charlotte?" she asked gently. "Have you remembered anything?"

I looked at her like a deer caught in a car's headlights, and I nodded as tears flowed from the corner of my eyes. I did not have the energy to sob but I let the sadness flow out of my body like blood flowing out of a wound. "My baby?" I whispered and I squeezed the nurse's hand, hopeful and desperate.

"I am so sorry, my darling, but you miscarried due to the injuries you had suffered."

I looked down at my body and saw that the heavy arm I was unable to lift was encased in a plaster cast. My eyes fell on my stomach and my free arm rested on it, clutching the blankets that covered my battered, broken body and I felt a piece of me die as my heart tore in two. I learned that I had four broken ribs, a broken arm, bruised kidneys and a fractured eye socket. I also had bruising to my back and stomach.

My mind shut down on me that day. Looking back, I guess it was the only way I could cope with the pain that I had been through.

I had to be forced to eat. I slept a lot or I cried a lot. I suffered anxiety, panic attacks and flashbacks about all of the arguments that Joe and I had had about the baby.

The baby. My baby. The baby that was going to change everything for the better and save us; or so I'd thought. The baby that was no longer a part of me, the baby that had been taken from me against my will.

Some people don't understand. They think that unless you are further on in your pregnancy, that it's not a baby, it is just a foetus and therefore it doesn't count. *Pull yourself together and get on with it. There'll always be another.* I'd heard people say things like that in the past but now that this had happened to me, I was able to see that you can't just pull yourself together when a part of you is missing. Some things can't be replaced.

My days were a blur of doctors trying to coax me into getting out of bed or eat a meal. I struggled to make sense of everything and felt as if I had been hit by a train. Emotionally I was shut down and I wasn't sure if I would ever be the same again.

The police came in to see me on two occasions. They first came the day after I woke up, and they asked me if I could remember what had happened on the night of the assault. I told them what I could remember and they informed me that because of the severity of the assault, they had taken out a police application for a domestic violence order against Joe. It was very confusing because they used a lot of terminology that I had never heard before, but the gist of it was that Joe was not allowed to hurt me within the two-year period of the order, and I could apply for extra conditions to stop him contacting me in person or by telephone, if I wanted to. The hospital had been advised not to allow Joe in to see me until I was strong enough to deal with the emotional trauma that I had experienced. They police also said that he would probably receive a short jail sentence because of the severity of my injuries.

I heard the nurses talking, saying that Joe tried every day to either see me or speak to me. I just felt numb when I heard that. I wasn't sure if I ever wanted to see him again but there was so much to think of with the houses. I wasn't very good at that kind of thing and he had taken care of the financial side of things, so I lay, wondering what to do feeling more overwhelmed than ever.

I still loved him but I was drowning in my grief and at the horror of what my life had become. I realized that there needed to be changes, I just wasn't strong enough to make them. My body was slowly healing but my mind felt fractured into pieces and I wondered if it would ever be whole again. So I lay in bed shutting out the voices of the doctors and nurses, rocking myself to sleep in the foetal position to try and stop the internal inferno of pain. I took as many pills as I could to numb me so that I didn't have to think. Oblivion was far better than the feeling of drowning in your own pain and grief.

CHAPTER 10

I had been in the hospital for almost seven days when I was told by the ward doctor, that I was being transferred to a psychiatric hospital. I should have felt shocked but sadly, I didn't. I knew that I needed help but I just wasn't sure if I wanted it. I was feeling stronger physically but I was still experiencing horrific flash backs and panic attacks.

I decided that I wanted see Joe. I was so unsure of how I felt that I needed to know where to go from here. I told the nurse when she came in with my pills and although she advised against it, she called him, and within forty minutes he was walking into my room. The nurse told me that they were propping the door open and would be able to see everything from their station that was situated directly outside of my room.

Joe looked at me and tears fell from his eyes but he remained silent. I hoped that it was tearing him apart inside and I hoped that the pain and suffering would stay with him forever. I took comfort in the fact that he was showing some remorse, which was reassuring.

He sat down next to the bed and looked at the floor.

"How are you?" he asked quietly, aware that we had an audience in the background. "Do I really have to answer that, Joe? I think you can see how I am by looking at me."

"I'm sorry OK Char, but you have no idea how much you wind me up. If you'd only kept your mouth shut."

I looked at him and despite loving him I realized that he would never change. He would never take responsibility for his actions. He would always blame me, or someone else, and things would always be this way. "I lost the baby," I said flatly, waiting for a look of regret or sadness or even the promise of trying again. "It's for the best, Charlotte. It was tearing us apart." He said without even flinching.

I snapped. "No, Joe. It wasn't the baby. The baby was the innocent victim in our charade of a marriage. The only thing tearing us apart is you, but you won't be doing that anymore because I've had it. I can't take any more. You're a bastard and a bully and you take pleasure from seeing me hurting and you need help, because you're not normal."

I was crying uncontrollably as I spat the words out at him. The nurse rushed in and ordered Joe to leave as the reality hit me and my marriage came crashing down around me, yet another brick in my ever growing wall of grief.

Joe was yelling out as he left the ward. "It's not over, Charlotte, and it never will be. You're mine! Mine, do you hear? No one else will ever have you."

The sound faded into the distance but the words hung in the air, floating around the room. I had a panic attack and gasped for breath as I clutched my chest, my head full of fear and looming death. The nurse gave me a sedative and I drifted into a restless void, which contained a mixture of reality and fiction, but I had difficulty separating which was which.

I was at St Wilfred's Hospital, which the locals referred to as the 'nut house'. At this stage I did not care. There was a stigma attached but I felt so unwell that I quite detached from the enormity of it. I had suffered a nervous breakdown and I had anxiety and post-traumatic stress disorder.

My cast was due to be removed and replaced by a splint. I just had to try and heal my heart and my mind now, which was proving easier said than done. The panic attacks that swamped me left me gasping for breath and fearing for my life. I would lose all grip on reality during those minutes that felt like hours. The aftermath of the panic attack was almost insufferable, as I sat waiting for the next one to hit; exhausted from the never-ending cycle. My body would tingle, I would get cramps and pains throughout my chest and convince myself that I was having a heart attack. My heart would race and I would sweat as hard as if I had just completed a marathon. I would have difficulty swallowing and I had a permanent feeling of nausea in the pit of my stomach.

The worst part, though, was the indescribable feeling of dread that would suddenly swoop upon me and turn my warm blood into icy cold liquid that would flow through my body sending fear to every single nerve ending.

I was jumpy and easily startled and I struggled to get a good night's sleep for fear of closing my eyes and seeing Joe. At times I would suffer flashbacks from the assaults and I would feel as if they were real. I was told that it would take time for the attacks to subside after experiencing on going violence. I was advised to up the dose of diazepam I was taking, in order to help control the levels of anxiety that I was experiencing.

Dr Pontin advised that I take part in daily yoga and meditation, as relaxation was a big part of my recovery. Dr Pontin was a man in his late fifties with a full head of wiry grey hair. He certainly looked like a classic example of a nutty professor. He had a very gentle approach and the most soothing voice I had ever heard. He promised me that I would get well and I believed him. He encouraged me to listen to CDs that were relaxing and he taught me breathing techniques so that when the panic attacks started I could try to control them. He arranged for me to have different types of holistic therapy treatments from Indian head massages, to reflexology and slowly but surely, I started to feel stronger.

Joe was constantly ringing my mobile and texting me. He would leave messages and swing from being apologetic and begging for forgiveness, to calling me every name under the sun. He would tell me that we could have a baby and then a few texts later he would be saying that he should have 'finished the fuckin job when he had the chance'.

He used to tell me when we lived together, that if I ever left him and went with another man, he would kill me and track me down, no matter where I was. It made a chill run through me just thinking about it and I felt more frightened than ever, because now that the relationship was over, he had nothing to lose and I worried that he would carry out his threat. He was unpredictable and violent and I was starting to think that he needed serious help. He had also turned up at the hospital earlier in the week, despite being told to keep away from me. I knew that I was supposed to report those breaches to the police but I felt so bad that he'd already been in so much trouble. I know that sounds crazy but I had developed a habit of feeling guilty, even when there was no logical reason for me to do so. I think it was a learnt behaviour because Joe had an uncanny knack of twisting everything and making *me* feel as if everything was always my fault. Even when I knew it didn't really make sense, he would be that convincing that I would find myself questioning my actions long after the event and feeling bad about it. I guess someone in that relationship had to have remorse and Joe certainly appeared to be devoid of that emotion.

I was waiting to find out if he had been sentenced and if so, for how long and it felt like the longest wait of my life. I knew he had done wrong, but I still loved him and a part of me would be devastated if he went to prison. I also feared what would happen when he got out. If he had been that mad over me calling him a bastard that he had beaten me to a pulp, I dreaded to think what he would do if he was sent to prison. I was under no illusions that he would blame me.

I had not told anyone that I was in hospital. The nurses had constantly asked me if there was anyone they could contact, but the only person I could think that I would want to see would be Nicki, and part of me wasn't ready to face her. The thought that I had been living a lie to her all this time would be difficult for her to understand, and I knew she would ask the question that I had asked myself every day since being in hospital, 'why did you stay?' I wish it was as easy as walking away, but I loved him so much and I always hoped that he would change, and there would be times when things were just the way they had been when we first met, and that was what I'd clung on to. Clearly, though, we had reached a point now where Joe had crossed a boundary and there was no way back.

Part of my therapy and recovery programme involved seeing a psychologist twice a week. Her name was Natalie and she looked to be in her early thirties, with shoulder length glossy brown hair and a stunning smile that lit up her face. At first I was nervous and I found it strange talking about everything after keeping it inside for so long, but Natalie had a way of making me feel at ease, and I found after two sessions that I was starting to really enjoy talking to her. The highlight for me was undoubtedly session ten. It had taken me weeks to tell my story because I kept breaking down and repeating myself, and it was a long story to tell. Natalie helped me understand what I had been through and clarified that it was not my fault.

"Charlotte, you have been the victim of extreme domestic violence. There is a pattern of power and control that abusers use. I am going to talk you through the different forms of abuse and I would like you to see if you can identify yourself as having experienced any."

She handed me a sheet and as I started to read through it, my mind started swirling with memories and thoughts associated with my past. I felt my face drain of colour as I realized that I could associate most of the things on that sheet with my relationship and marriage to Joe.

Physical abuse – Hitting/punching, choking, hair pulling, burning, kicking, using weapons or objects to harm.

Psychological Abuse – playing mind games, minimizing concerns, ignoring feelings or placing blame.

Financial Abuse – Controlling and withholding money – restricting activities and necessities.

Verbal Abuse – Name calling, using words to instil fear, degrading or derogatory remarks.

Sexual Abuse – forcing partner to engage in sexual activities against their will, rape, withholding of birth control pills.

Intimidation – Imposing fear by using looks, or gestures, threatening to harm children or pets, destroying possessions.

Using privilege – Using culture, religion or gender to impose authority.

Isolation – Monitoring phone calls, limiting contact with friends or family, encouraging moves to remote areas.

I looked up at Natalie for a few seconds before looking back to the sheet. I felt drawn to it like a magnet to metal. I could not pull my eyes away from the words that swam in front of me as my eyes filled with tears, tears of shock and relief. I felt as if someone had just shaken me back to life and I was able to see things more clearly.

"Charlotte, how does it feel to look at that sheet?"

"To be honest, it feels overwhelming. There is a part of me that is in total shock, and there's a part of me that feels relieved that what I have been through has a title, so to speak. The things he told me, the way he belittled me and put me down, it was all about power and control. Does this mean that I am not mad after all?"

"I very much doubt that you have ever been mad, Charlotte. That was all part of the domestic abuse.

Perpetrators convince their partners that they are crazy or stupid. They belittle them and undermine them in an attempt to shatter their self-confidence. They manipulate and take control so that you start to doubt everything about yourself and become dependent on them. There is a form of mental abuse called 'gas lighting'. Abusers will deny saying and doing things and play mind games, all with the intention of making the victim feel like they are losing their memory or going insane. It can be very confusing when you have witnessed someone do something and they then stand there and adamantly deny it, and when someone is so convincing about something being all your fault, you eventually start to believe them."

"So all of the times when Joe told me I was crazy, he was just messing with my head? All the comments about the way I looked and dressed and the things that he denied doing or saying was a part of this game he was playing?"

"Joe's behaviour certainly fits in with the pattern of domestic violence and power and control. However I doubt that Joe would agree with that. Research has shown that abusers rarely take responsibility for their behaviour. In the beginning of the relationship they tend to follow a pattern of remorse after an abusive incident. However, this can quickly diminish with time, with abusers eventually showing little regret for their abuse. Often men do not realize that emotional and psychological abuse *is* actual abuse. They usually follow a pattern with friends and work colleagues, their boss

170

etc., where they refuse to admit when they are in the wrong. They can go to great lengths to justify their behaviour, always ending with it being someone else's fault. In their eyes they often see themselves as the victim and blame someone else for pushing them over the edge. Quite often they can be replicating behaviour that they experienced during their childhood, a learnt behaviour. They are almost switched off to it and do not form a link between their childhood experiences and their adult behaviour. Do you know much about Joe's childhood Charlotte?"

"I'm embarrassed to say I don't. He rarely talked about his parents. I've met them several times but they seemed to have a distant relationship and Joe just said that they weren't close. He never really expanded on that."

"Maybe we will never know and either way it is irrelevant, because nothing excuses his behaviour. I would like you to look at this pattern of behaviour Charlotte which is the cycle of violence."

I looked down at the sheet and started reading.

The Honeymoon Phase – Denial of previous abuse. Everything is calm and the abuser is charming and loving, often planning far into the future. This gives the victim hope that everything will change for the better.

The build-up phase – This is when tension starts to build and the victim's anxiety levels may start increasing.

Intimidation Phase – The abuser becomes more controlling and intimidating and the victim usually feels afraid of the abuser at this stage.

Explosion – The abuser hits/hurts or abuses the victim.

The Remorse Phase – The abuser is either remorseful and promises that it will never happen again, or they minimalize the abuse, often blaming the victim.'

The pursuit Phase – Pursuit of promises (I'll change/seek help). Helplessness, (without you I am nothing). Threats (I might as well kill myself if I can't have you/if I can't have you no one will).

Again I could see that there had been a pattern in the relationship.

"What are you thinking right now?" Natalie asked gently, after allowing me time to read through it and reflect.

"I'm thinking that I should have been able to see this pattern myself, but it's strange, because I didn't. I almost feel like I must have been living in a bubble, because how was I not able to see what was right in front of me? Now that I look back it is so obvious, but at the time - well, I don't know. I just didn't see it. I guess my love for him and fear of losing him blinded me."

"This is the thing about domestic violence that a lot of people don't understand. When you first start a relationship it is easy to confuse control with love. The fact that Joe was so loving and attentive and proposed within such a short span of time is also typical of a potential abuser, but to you, he was in love with you and you with him. The relationship was fast paced and intoxicating to the point of almost being addictive.

Usually, in the early stages of the abuse, after a blow up or assault, a partner might threaten to leave or end the relationship. This causes panic because by that stage you are usually in love with them; and because it has only happened the once or twice, you are convinced that you can work things out. That in itself becomes a problem, though, as you start second guessing if and when they might leave, and insecurities can build significantly, leaving you feeling vulnerable and uncertain of your future. People assume it is easy to walk away and we live in a society with an attitude of, 'Why don't they just leave?' in regard to domestic violence. It's not that easy. If an abuser punched you on the first or second date you would end that relationship immediately. What people don't understand is that the abuse is subtle and it builds up in time. Typically, by the time that you realize things aren't great, you are in love with that person and usually isolated from friends and family. Your self-esteem may be rock bottom as well, and it's not a case of just walking out. Abusers are very good at making their victims think that they can't live without them."

"That is so true. I feel that now I am out of it and I can look back, it is so glaringly obvious. However, at the time I was just living from day to day. It makes me even more afraid of Joe, and I know that he has been trying to see me because the nurses have told me. He has also

173

been texting me repeatedly so he has little regard for the domestic violence order that the police took out. I don't want to see him. I can't, because I know that he will convince me to go back and I just can't because I -"

I start to cry.

****

Our next session was more focused as I had spent time reflecting on everything and absorbing the information that Natalie had given me.

"Have a seat, Charlotte. How are you feeling today?" She asked.

"I feel a bit stronger, thanks. I am still having panic attacks but they are not as frequent and the new medication that Dr Pontin put me on seems to be helping."

"Have you given any thought to what you will do when you leave hospital? What are your plans regarding Joe? Do you intend to go back to him?"

I sat and thought for a while. I knew that I had been lucky to walk away from that assault and it had made me realize that I needed to get out of the relationship permanently, despite the fact that I still loved Joe. "I have to leave but to be honest, I am so scared of him finding me I just don't know what to do. I can't imagine him allowing me to get on with my life and the thought of him turning up to my house and hurting me or constantly causing scenes is unbearable."

"Do you have any family or friends that you could stay with? I agree that you are at extreme risk, especially given his previous threats to kill you if you ever leave him, I really do think that you would be better off staying with someone. I know the police have taken out a domestic violence order against him but he has breached that several times already by turning up at the hospital. We need to do some safety planning around your future because the most risky time for a victim is once they have left. I say victim, Charlotte, because that is what the literature in DV reports state, but I prefer to think of you as a survivor."

"I have family in Scarborough but Joe knows that. I also have family in Australia and I have thought a lot about them the past week or so. I telephoned my aunt and she has told me that I am more than welcome to stay with them for as long as I want. They live in a place called Toowoomba, which is an hour or so outside of Brisbane in Queensland. I think I might take some time out and move there for a while to put some space between Joe and I and give myself time to heal properly. I say heal, but I'm not sure I will ever get over what he put me through, however, I think it will be good for me to have that space and feel safe. I'm sure that will help me get well again."

"That sounds like a great idea. How about I ask one of the hospital support staff to assist you with practical issues such as getting information about visas, printing forms off etc.? If nothing else, it will give you a bit of a head start and you definitely deserve a break after everything you've been through."

"That would be great, Natalie, thanks so much. If you hadn't had an understanding of domestic violence I would probably have left here and gone straight back to Joe. The more I have thought about it all, the more it makes sense and the better I feel, just knowing that it wasn't my fault."

I found out one day prior to being released from hospital that Joe had been sentenced to eight weeks in jail for his assault on me. Part of me felt that this was a bit severe, but Natalie reminded me that he could have killed me and almost did. I worried that if he lost his job, he would come out of prison angrier than ever. However, I was relieved that he was out of the way because it meant that I could go to the house and get my passport, clothes, and the personal items that I planned on taking with me.

I left St Wilfred's hospital with my repeat prescriptions for anti-anxiety medication and I agreed to continue weekly counselling sessions with Natalie until I left the country.

Even though my house was empty, I could not face sleeping there as there were too many memories, so I booked myself into a hotel. I knew that I needed to go back there and get my belongings so I dropped off the few pieces that I had with me at the hotel, and took a taxi there.

I felt shaky and nervous as I turned the key, and I half expected Joe to jump out from behind one of the doors. I stood looking at the house and realized that I hated that house and all of the memories that it held. It had always felt like Joe's house, because he was the one who had wanted it. I would have settled for something much less grand.

I took my passport, birth certificate, marriage certificate, a copy of the mortgage agreement and I stuffed them into my bag. Then I filled a box with photographs of my family, jewellery and hairdryer and cosmetics. I went into the spare bedroom and crammed as many clothes and shoes as I could fit into two suitcases. I climbed into the attic, all the while listening out for any noises, fearful that Joe would be waiting when I turned around. It was silly because I knew that he was in prison, but I guess it's like living with an evil shadow, everywhere you turn, you are reminded of a memory and the shadow stays with you, haunting you daily.

I grabbed the box of things that my mum and dad had kept from my childhood. There was a teddy bear that my nana and granddad had bought me when I was born: books, a scrapbook from my first holiday abroad and a few other bits and pieces that had sentimental value. There was nothing else I wanted because nothing in that house had any meaning to me anymore. I loaded them into the boot of the taxi and returned to the hotel.

I booked an appointment with the solicitor for the following day and I had decided to file for divorce on the grounds of unreasonable behaviour. The police had told me that the domestic violence order against Joe would work in my favour. My next big decision was that I had decided to sell my parents' house. It was too painful for me to keep it and I could not imagine myself returning to Alnmouth. It was too small a village and I would constantly bump into Joe. Despite what he had done to me, I still could not stand the thought of seeing him with another woman. I also wanted to sell the house that we had bought together. I knew that Joe didn't have the money to buy me out but I would never live in that house after everything that had happened. I needed a fresh break and a new start.

The following morning I walked into John Towart's office and he stood up from his desk to greet me.

"Hi Charlotte. What can I do for you my dear?" He asked with his trademark spectacles hanging off the end of his nose.

I told him the story as briefly as I could, covering everything that I felt was of importance. He listened, and then let out a long sigh as he ran his fingers through his hair. "Charlotte, I am horrified about what you have been through. I have known your family for years, as you know. I will do my best to support you through this."

"Thank you. I think I am going to Australia to visit family and to take a break away from this place. I know that Joe won't let me move forward with my life and he won't give up without a fight. I don't have the strength to deal with that any more, it's exhausting. I want to file for divorce on grounds of his unreasonable behaviour and I have a copy here of his domestic violence order. I would also like to sell my parents' house and the house that Joe and I bought together, but I am not sure how I go about that. Am I able to do that from Australia or do I have to stay in the country?"

"I think going to Australia for some time out is a very good decision, Charlotte. What I will do is draw up as much paperwork as possible before you leave. You can come in and sign it all and any signatures that we need at a later date, can easily be done via email. All you will have to do is print, sign and then scan the documents and return them to me. When do you plan on leaving?"

"I am just waiting on my holiday visa coming through, really. Can you call me as soon as you have drafted what is needed and I will call back in to the office? Joe gets released from prison in five weeks' time so I am keen to be gone by then."

"Yes, of course, I understand. I will be in touch early next week. In the meantime, I will notify Mr Porter about the divorce and the imminent house sale. I am aware that he may not receive the letter until he has been released from prison, but I agree that it is in your best interests not to hang around here."

****

179

The next few weeks were spent in a flurry of activity. My working holiday visa for Australia arrived three weeks after I sent the application in! Everything was moving so quickly that I didn't have time to stop and think about the enormity of what I was doing, but I felt that this was a good thing because if I had stopped and thought about it, I might have changed my mind and then there would be no escaping Joe. I knew that I would always love him, despite what he had put me through.

I wrote a letter to Nicki, explaining everything and telling her that I would be in touch as soon as I could. I did not tell her where I was going because I knew that Joe would ask her at some stage and I didn't want to put her in that position. He was still sending me text messages on a daily basis, mostly he was telling me that he was sorry and that he had learnt his lesson. I wanted to believe him so badly, but I knew even being around him would send my anxiety levels through the roof and I would never be able to trust him, and I would always be waiting for him to blow up and assault me again. Now that we were no longer together I felt as if I could breathe. It felt as if a veil of suffocation had been lifted from me and it felt good. I hated him for destroying me, for making me think that I was ugly, skinny and useless. I hated that he had accused me of things that I had never done and I hated the fact that he had hurt me and hit me. But most of all I hated that he had killed our baby and shown no remorse. He was a bully and a manipulative, nasty, jealous man and distance from him allowed me to see that clearly now. I pitied the next woman who would have to live with that because I doubted that he would change. Everything was always about his needs and wants and even though it still hurt when I thought of him or pictured him in my head, I was pleased to be free of that tormented hell that I had lived through because of him.

CHAPTER 11

Over the next few weeks I felt extremely lonely, despite having a lot to organise. I was so used to Joe and his suffocating ways, always cooking for him or having to text him and try to keep him happy, that I wasn't sure what to do with myself when I was alone.

In hospital I had spent most of my time regaining strength, sleeping a lot, doing yoga and different therapy groups and sessions. Now I was suddenly free and all alone and it felt so alien to me.

I spent most of my days at the library, researching Australia and constantly checking flight prices and times. I was emailing Aunt Susan almost daily by this stage and I was careful what I said to her. Obviously she knew that I was married because she had been invited to the wedding so I told her that the marriage was over and that I needed to get away. She never pushed for information, which I was relived about. I wasn't sure I could face getting there and being interrogated.

I spent some time every second day visiting my parents' grave. I know it sounds silly, but I found talking out loud to them really helpful.

I sat on the grass next to the headstone and checked that no one else was around before I spoke out loud.

"I know you're both not here but, well, I kinda feel that you can hear me. I am so sorry for letting you down and not being wiser and stronger. I never thought that I would end up in this situation. I struggle some days to make sense of it all. I ask myself when it all started did I miss something huge? Should I have left after the first assault? Should I have listened to Nicki? I could literally torture myself, but I guess I am where I am now, and I really hope that you understand why I have to get away from here. It breaks my heart that I won't be able to come here and put fresh flowers in the vase, but I will put artificial ones in before I leave. I will never stop loving you both and if you can hear me, all I ask is that you give me your blessing and send me some strength to get through this, because some days I feel as if it is all too much. If I could have one wish, it would be to have you both here and I guess home just doesn't feel like home anymore without you. There's nothing left for me here. Ok, so I'm going now before I start sobbing again. Love you both to the moon and back and more."

****

I had started reading self-help books and despite still experiencing anxiety, I was feeling stronger than I had in a while. I still had flashbacks of the assaults, but that was mainly at night when I tried to sleep so I practised meditation and although I found it hard to focus my mind, I was slowly getting the hang of it. I think one of the most valuable lessons I had learned in hospital was to take care of me and be OK with that. I still had the nagging voices of doubt sitting on my shoulder, ready to validate all of the things Joe had said to me. When I tried outfits on I found myself wondering if I looked too skinny and I would often look at myself in the mirror, wondering if I was ugly. Some days were better than others, and on a bad day I would look at myself and cry and on a good day I would think that I looked fine. I had a feeling that it would take a long time to get rid of those voices, and some days I wondered if I ever would.

I was back and forward to the solicitors, signing papers so that I could proceed with the divorce and the house could go up for sale, and then two weeks before Joe's release I received a message from him.

Someone had obviously been in the house and taken mail to him. The text message ranted on for pages and pages. The gist of it was that he was saying he would not sell the house and that I could go fuck myself, and that he was not agreeing to a divorce. He ended it by saying I would be sorry for this whole mess and who the fuck did I think I was to try and make him homeless and penniless, and to watch my back and make sure I didn't close my eyes too tight while sleeping. I broke down. All

I was doing was trying to move on and escape the horror and I was still stuck in the living nightmare. I took the phone to the police and showed them the message. The police printed a copy off the phone and told me that they would be charging Joe with a breach of his domestic violence order. I felt relieved that they were doing something about it, but it also added to my heightened sense of anxiety about his release. I booked myself in with Natalie for one final session before I left for Australia.

I spent the session talking about the recent contact I had had from Joe. I talked about my fear of him trying to track me down if I stayed in the area, and I agreed that it would be liberating to feel free and safe in Australia. There was no way Joe would ever think to find me there and more importantly, he didn't know where my aunt lived.

I came out of my session with Natalie feeling much more focused and I went to the travel agent to book a flight to Brisbane. As I handed over my bank card to pay for the flight, I felt exhilarated at the thought of being free but terrified at the same time. I had five days left before I flew out of England to start my new life.

Next stop was the Post Office, where I arranged for all of my post to be forwarded on to Australia, and then I went to the bank to transfer money.

I made my way back to the hotel room, picked up my phone book and started calling friends and the little family that I had left. I called Jimmy first and he was adorable as always. He asked no questions and just wished me all the best for the future and asked me to send him the odd postcard, just so he knew that I was safe and well. Lastly I called my aunt Trish. I hesitated before typing in the number because I knew I would get the third degree from her, but I punched the last digit in and waited.

"Hi, Aunty Trish. How are you?"

"Oh, Charlotte, my lovely, how are you? Are you bearing up, love? I have rung the house so many times but I always seem to get the answer machine."

"Yes, well, it's a little awkward, but that is why I am ringing you. You see, Joe and I have separated. I've left him."

"Whatever for, darling girl? Oh, and he's so handsome. Why would you want to leave? And I mean, you're married for goodness' sake. This makes no sense to me whatsoever."

I took a deep breath before replying. "Joe used to hit me, Aunt Trish. I've just got out of hospital. It's really hard for me and if you don't mind, I don't really want to say any more than that. I'm calling because things are pretty bad and it's best for me to get away for a while, so I'm going to Australia to stay with Dad's sister, Susan. I just wanted to let you know."

"Oh, my goodness. As if you haven't been through enough. He seemed like such a nice young lad as well. It's all a bit of a shock though. I mean - how long -"
"Sorry, Aunt Trish, I have to go. I am leaving in a few

days so I just called to let you know and once I get there I will send you a postcard to let you know that I am safe and well. Love to everyone. Sorry, I have to dash. Bye."

I slammed the phone down as if it was burning hot. My heart was hammering. I knew she would try to interrogate me even though I'd asked her not too. I sat down and took some deep breaths.

I had toyed with the idea of phoning Joe's parents but then I had asked myself what that would achieve? It would only make him all the more angry and I wasn't even sure if they would be that bothered, so I had decided against it.

****

My last day in the area was a strange one. I felt nervous as I drove around and looked at all of the buildings. I watched people walking down the street, people that I had known most of my life, even if only by sight. I drove past my parents' house and then parked outside *our* house. I walked to the bottom of the street and took the alley towards the river. I crossed the wooden bridge and sat under the very tree that I had sat at on the night that Joe had told me to 'get rid' of our baby. I looked over at the house and all its splendour. From the outside, you could never imagine people living in unhappiness or fear inside of those solid stonewalls. From the outside it looked almost perfect, however, I knew different. I would not be sad to walk away from what I had had, not the material things anyway. They didn't matter. I was still devastated and heartbroken that the man I had married turned out to be such a monster. There had been so many good times in the beginning. I had loved spending time with him, planning our future and sharing ideas and just listening to him, and being around him had been enough, I had never really wanted much more than that. Now I doubted that I would ever trust another man again.

I hadn't bothered arranging a meet up with any of the girls that I used to work with. Joe had ensured that I had as few friends as possible. People eventually stop asking when you decline time and time again, so I spent the rest of the day taking photographs of the things that I would miss when I was in Australia.

I sat overlooking the river, eating fish and chips smothered in salt and vinegar and I tried to picture myself one week from now. It was such a strange feeling, trying to imagine myself in a country that I had never been to. I imagined that because we spoke the same language that it would be quite similar to England, just with sunshine. I wondered what I would be doing this time next week and how I would be feeling.

I had made sure that I had enough medication to last me several months and planned on taking a diazepam just before I boarded the plane. Hopefully that would knock me out for some of the flight. I had only ever flown as far as Spain, which was only two hours away. This flight in total was taking twenty five hours!

I bought myself some magazines and a book to help keep me entertained on the plane. I had a seven-hour flight to Dubai, with a four-hour stopover, which would give me just enough time to have a look around the airport. I would then be flying direct to Brisbane which would take approximately fourteen hours. I would have loved to stop over in Dubai for a few days to explore the city but I was too afraid to do anything like that on my own. Getting on the plane to Australia would be the bravest thing I had done in my life!

I double checked that I had everything that I needed; passport, tickets, purse and money. I had my most precious jewellery in a pouch inside my handbag. I threw a bikini, flip flops, sun cream and kaftan in the suitcase and squashed the clothes down so that I could zip it up.

I got into bed for the last time in England and I lay staring at the ceiling for what felt like forever. Ironic that tonight was the one night I needed to sleep well, considering I was going to be awake for the next twenty-five plus hours.

I eventually drifted off to sleep. I dreamt that I was walking on a beach and I turned around to see a kangaroo behind me in the distance. It steadily hopped behind me, keeping a good distance as I walked, enjoying the feeling of the sun on my skin and the warm sand between my toes. I turned around and the kangaroo had closed the gap between us and I started to feel nervous. The next time I looked it was bouncing towards me and then suddenly everything changed and it was Joe running at me. His eyes were as black as onyx and his face was twisted and angry and he was making a screaming sound that ripped through my body, causing waves of fear to crash through me. I started to run but I kept stumbling on the sand. I tripped repeatedly and got back up again and all the while Joe was gaining speed and shortening the distance between us. I was terrified and could feel my heart hammering in my chest. Fighting through layers of sleep to consciousness, I woke up with sweat dripping off me, and a throat as dry as sun-bleached sand. I looked around and saw that I was in the hotel room and I was safe. My breathing was rapid, as was my heartbeat. It was five ten am so I decided to get up, get showered and dressed. My flight was at ten thirty, so I had to be at the airport for eight thirty. I tried to steady my nerves by doing ten minutes of meditation. I knew it was crazy but I had an overwhelming fear of Joe turning up at the airport.

My taxi pulled up and I loaded my suitcase into the boot. I sat quietly for most of the journey, contemplating what I had been through and wondering what lay ahead. I felt my stomach somersault when I saw the airport, but determinedly I walked through the automatic doors and looked around for the desk that I needed. I was early and still had to wait ten minutes so I grabbed a coffee and sandwich from the shop and by the time I had walked back to the check in, it was open and a small queue had formed. I handed over my passport and e-ticket when I got to the desk, and waited while the glamorous girl behind the counter weighed my luggage.

Eventually I boarded the plane and I was relieved to see that I had a row of three seats to myself. I looked out of the window as we taxied down the run way and I had an overwhelming urge to cry, but I knew that it would draw attention, so I closed my eyes until I felt the tears recede. I swallowed the lump in my throat and quietly said goodbye to Newcastle upon Tyne.

I landed at Dubai airport seven hours later and was mesmerized by the glittering gold jewellery and designer shops. There were women walking around in their traditional dress of hijab and long black robes that covered their bodies. They entered the designer shops and some came out laden with bags. I could not imagine owning such expensive clothing only to have to hide them under a long robe.

I moved seats once we were on our way to Brisbane. I moved to a row of empty seats so that I would get a chance to stretch out and sleep if I wanted to. I watched a movie and then settled myself down with a pillow propped against the armrest and a blanket draped over me. I closed my eyes and drifted off into a land filled with sand that glittered like gold, oceans that were as transparent as glass, and a sun that filled the whole sky with orange and yellow hues.

I was on my way to Australia.

CHAPTER 12

Arriving in Australia was a surreal experience. I landed in Brisbane at six am after a journey totalling almost thirty hours.

I was exhausted and felt a mixture of anticipation and relief. I felt nervous about staying with relatives that I barely knew, and nervous about being in a foreign country, but I felt huge relief that Joe would not be turning up at my door or harassing me and I felt myself relax for the first time in a long time.

I stepped off the plane to be met by the blazing heat from the engines and the enormous Australian sun. I had only ever been to Spain twice when I was younger, so this was a huge adventure for me.

The floor felt as if it was moving beneath me and I guessed that jetlag and lack of sleep were to blame, and although the flight itself had been fine I had been unable to sleep. I had tried to watch movies, I'd tried reading, but I just couldn't concentrate. I had too much going through my mind.

I snapped out of my daydreaming when the carousel jerked to life and suitcases started chugging around the belt. I grabbed my case and headed through the doors. I saw Uncle Will standing with a sign with my name in bold letters, and I smiled despite my nerves. I had only spoke to Uncle Will a few times on Skype and now here I was, about to move into his house. I felt a wave of nausea wash over me as nerves changed to outright fear and doubt about whether I had made the right decision.

"Uncle Will?" I asked quietly. "G'day, Charlotte. How are you?" he asked in a loud Aussie accent as he gave me a hug and a man-sized pat on the back. "Come, let's get you home. Your Aunt Suze is in the house prettying the place up for you and baking enough food to feed a bloody army." He laughed and I felt embarrassed at his loudness, but no one else around me seemed to even notice.

We headed out of Brisbane and I suddenly felt wide awake. I looked around at all of the high rise buildings and I was surprised at how green and leafy the place looked. For some reason I had thought that Australia would be all dry, barren, dusty land.

We headed west and the land became dryer the further west we went. "Oh, wow, there's a kangaroo," I shouted excitedly!

Uncle Will laughed. "That's a wallaby, Charlotte. You'll soon learn the difference." He said confidently.

We turned onto a dusty drive way and pulled up at the house, which I soon learnt was a Queenslander. It looked very grand from the outside, with a large balcony that spread around the whole of the top floor. It was made of wood and painted white, and it looked so very different to the houses back home.

My aunt Susan ran out to greet me. "Aunt Susan," I said as I hugged her, feeling my worries melt away. "Now I think we are both old enough for you to call us Susan and Will. No need for the aunt and uncle title here." She held me at arm's length and looked at me. "You're the double of your mum, sweet girl. I am so sorry about what happened. How are you coping?"

I decided to wait a while before telling her the whole story, so I nodded as my eyes brimmed with tears.

"This is just the place you need to be to heal, darling girl. You'll never want to leave, gets hold of your soul, Australia does." She hugged me again and jostled me forwards, towards the house.

The house was refreshingly different when I stepped inside. We went down the stairs, where there was a bedroom and bathroom to the right of the room and a large rumpus room which took up the main area. There was an old, comfortable looking sofa and a floor lamp and a bookcase. A fragile looking desk stood against the wall with a computer that must have been at least twenty years old. The upper floor and main part of the house had a large lounge area, a kitchen and two large bedrooms plus another bathroom. The furniture was old fashioned compared to the UK but it somehow suited the house. The kitchen benches were full of plates of food.

Pies, sausage rolls, homemade scones and biscuits and despite not feeling hungry, my mouth was watering at the thought of the home baked treats.

In the far corner of the room there was a table with lace tablecloth and a vase full of fresh flowers, which filled the room with a heady, delicious scent. A bookcase stuffed with a variety of books stood against the back wall and double wooden doors opened out onto the huge veranda. The upper floor was so bright and filled with positive energy, and for the first time in months I felt thankful that I was alive.

The veranda had a hammock, swinging gently in the breeze at one end and there was possibly the biggest barbeque I'd ever seen standing against the wall. At the other end two double wicker sofas sat opposite each other with a small table in between.

The view from the back of the balcony was magnificent. On the left side of the house you had the landscape in the distance, with tree covered hills and grassy flats with horses and cows grazing, and on the deck leading directly out of the kitchen there were the views of the beautiful and expansive garden. There was a mixture of orange, lemon and apple trees. There were coconut palms with large green coconuts hanging from them, causing the fronds to sag heavily. Eight banana plants stood opposite each other in a row of four, like soldiers in a parade, and various other trees and flowers swayed in the gentle breeze. The smell was intoxicating.

At the very back of the garden there was a generous vegetable patch planted with potatoes, carrots, onions and leeks. Half a dozen chickens scratched around in the dirt while several sat inside a chicken coop, out of the intense morning sun. I was amazed at people having chickens in their back garden but Will assured me that it was quite the thing here.

"Wow, your garden is amazing, Will," I said, as he stood alongside me puffing away on his cigarette. "Yup, it sure is. When me and Suze moved here years ago there were only a few shops. It was cheaper to grow your own food, and to be honest, the taste is much better. I've got me chooks that lay our eggs for breakfast and Suze does a great lemon drizzle cake with those lemons." He nodded in the direction of the fruit trees.

I almost laughed when he said chooks. Will had a carefree attitude about him and I found it quite refreshing. He was straight up. No airs and graces, just a genuine, real person. I could see why Susan had fallen for that thirty years ago. "We thought that you could have the basement, Charlotte, but join us for meals, of course," Susan said as she stepped onto the veranda with a tray full of food and drinks. "That way you will have some space of your own. What do you think?"

"That would be great, Susan. I am so grateful to you both for making me so welcome."

Susan came up and hugged me tightly. "And we are so happy to have you here, dear girl. I am not sure what you have been through but I'm sure you will tell us when you are ready. For now you can get some good home cooked food into you. You look like you could do with fattening up a little." She smiled as she said it but I still felt that stab of hurt, as it reminded me of the painful and nasty remarks that Joe used to make.

After I had filled myself with Susan's delicious food I took my suitcase downstairs and hung my clothes up in the wardrobe. I was exhausted but I knew if I went to sleep now, I would be awake half of the night.

It was peaceful down here. I had a large window, which let in a surprising amount of light, so I opened it up and a warm breeze swirled through the room bringing with it a mixture of scent from the garden. There was no TV down here but I quite liked that because it meant I could use this space as my chill out room, a room where I could relax.

I decided to go for a walk with Susan in an effort to keep myself awake, and I was eager to get to know the area a little better.

It was almost one pm and the sun was beating down on us. I had covered myself in cream before leaving the house and I was glad of it because I could feel the sun nipping at my skin within minutes of setting off.

The house was on a small incline with a long, dusty, winding road and if you didn't know where you were going, you would probably drive straight by, unaware that a house was hidden behind the trees that circled the property. The rusty old letterbox placed at the bottom of the road was the only sign that there was someone living close by. I would never have felt safe enough back home living on such a remote property, but here it felt natural.

We walked around the curve in the road and Susan pointed out the way to the main shops, which were within walking distance, although I wasn't sure that I'd be offering to do that trip very often in this heat. It was thirty-three degrees and I feared that I would resemble a cooked lobster if I stayed out in the heat for too long.

We walked a fair distance and came across something that I had never seen before; a drive-through bottle shop. It was an amusing sight to see people driving through and loading up their cars with bottles of wine and cases of beer. "The Aussies like their grog," Susan said with a smile. "They work hard so they like to wind down at the end of the day with a nice cold beer or glass of wine. It's surprising how you get used to the changes in lifestyle. Just you wait and see."

I smiled but still felt such a mixture of emotions. I decided to head back to the house and go to bed after a light meal. I was exhausted and felt like sleeping on my feet. If I did rise early I would watch the sun come up on the veranda.

And that was exactly what I did the following day. I woke up at four am. I put the lamp on next to the bed and read a few chapters of my book before getting dressed. I made myself a cup of green tea, I picked a lemon from the tree in the garden and added a slice to my steaming cup and I sat down on the padded wicker sofa on the veranda. I heard Will rise just before the sun came up. I sat with my mug of tea and watched as the world changed before my eyes. Everything came alive with the rising of the sun. Several chooks ran out of their coop, birds made noises unlike anything I'd heard before as they flew from tree to tree. A large white cockatoo landed on the veranda and pecked its way along the wooden deck in search of a few titbits, and kookaburras laughed together in the trees surrounding the house. I stayed there until the sun was high enough up to warm me through and I closed my eyes, savouring the moment. It felt so surreal.

Who would have thought I would have been sitting in Australia watching the sunrise? I felt incredibly blessed when I considered where my life had been at, only seven weeks earlier.

****

I kept in touch with my solicitor regularly and he informed me that Joe had been released from prison. Reluctantly, he had agreed to sell the house, but he was still contesting the divorce.

The next few months passed in a blur. I spent some time getting to know the area, but mostly stayed out of the living world by going for walks, tending the trees and plants and collecting veggies from the garden. I had even learned to go in the chicken house to collect eggs.

I started learning to drive, and I was surprised at how much I was enjoying it. Will and Susan took turns in taking me out for lessons on the weekends and I felt confident enough to sit my test after four months. I passed first time and Susan and Will invited some friends around to their house for a barbeque and beers; and that was how I ended up falling into my first job in Australia.

Bob was a local guy who ran a machinery hire firm. He offered me a job in admin because I had some experience. Personally, I thought the numerous cans of lager had had more to do with it, but he was true to his word and came back the following day to give me a rundown on when I was starting and what my working hours would be.

I felt so nervous the first day that I pulled up at BRB Machinery in town. Susan had dropped me off thirty minutes early, as she was a firm believer in making a good impression and I sensed that she did not want to feel let down by me, because Bob was a friend. My anxiety levels were quite high the first month. I felt nervous meeting new people and constantly wondered if I was up to the job, but because I had little else to focus on it soon became my obsession. I loved having a reason to get out of bed in the morning. I loved earning my own money and took pleasure in contributing to the household bills, despite Susan and Will insisting that they did not want any money off me.

During my lunch break I would take a list of machinery outside with me while I ate, and I would scan through it again and again, until I had memorized all of the machines. I loved doing a job and doing it well because it gave me a sense of pride and slowly my confidence started to return, although I doubted that it would ever be the same again.

My biggest challenge was my accent. Some people loved it but others would ask me to repeat what I was saying, time and time again. I was never quite sure if they struggled to understand what I was saying or whether they were laughing at me. However, it was all part of the experience and I learned to hide my nerves and take it in my stride.

Bob told me I was doing a great job and promoted me to team leader after four months. One of the older women who worked there was clearly unhappy about me being offered the position and she made it well known and would mutter, 'Bloody Poms' under her breath just loud enough for me to hear. I ignored her. I was starting to get a bit of a tougher skin these days and wasn't so accepting of people pushing me around or taking advantage. I didn't go about things in an aggressive way I simply addressed whatever problem there was, calmly and head on.

Time flew by and before I knew it I had been in Australia for six months. I missed home and the familiarity of places most of all, and I was finding homesickness a strange and unpleasant experience. I could go for weeks, or even a month or more and feel fine and then, without warning, a feeling of anxiety and extreme longing would envelop me and leave me reeling. I would want nothing more than to book a flight and step on a plane back home. Sometimes the feeling lasted hours: other times, days. I wanted to crawl under the duvet and hide away from the world on those days. If it hadn't been for the fear of Joe, I think I would have returned during one of those homesick episodes, because when they hit, I could not think of anything positive about Australia, no matter how much I wanted to. The sun felt too hot, the noisy birds irritated me, the calmness and stillness of the place became boring and I felt lost in a country bigger than the whole of Europe. But as suddenly as homesickness encased me, it would leave and I would find myself listening out for the different bird songs, and the quiet of the land as I sat enjoying the heat of the sun on my now bronzed skin.

I received an email from the estate agents in early July to say that a couple wanted buy my parents' house. I accepted immediately, despite the offer being a little lower that I had hoped for. I also heard from my solicitor that Joe was still refusing to sign any paperwork in relation to the divorce, so it looked like I would have to wait a while before I was no longer married to him. I still missed him and often thought about him, about the good times. Sadly, though, I realized that most of them had been earlier on in the relationship, because almost as soon as we married he changed.

There were times when I felt blessed that I lived here, and there were times when I felt lost in some strange void, neither wanting to stay, nor go home. I tried to take one day at a time, though, and enjoy the freedom of not having to answer to anyone.

Work was going well and I was really enjoying my role as team leader. After one of our weekly team meetings, Bob asked me to stay back. He told me that he was expanding the business and that he had just signed a lease on an office block at Kangaroo Point, Brisbane.

The plan was that Bob would open the office within the next three months and he wanted me to go in as head of human resources. I was blown away and very flattered, but also conscious of the responsibility and nervous as to whether I was up to it. After all, it was a big step up from my current role. However, I had little else to fill my time with so I felt that it was too good of an opportunity to turn down and it would be a challenge. However, I wasn't so sure about moving to Brisbane. I could commute daily, but because it was a one and a half hour drive it would mean a very long working day. I could catch the train but it wasn't completely reliable, so the best option all round would be for me to find an apartment to lease. I had saved a lot of money because Susan and Will refused to take money off me. I bought groceries and put money in the jar toward the electric bill, but I still had little else to spend my money on. Susan suggested that we could spend a weekend in Brisbane and the surrounding areas and have a look at a few apartments to get an idea of prices. It would also give us a chance to do some shopping and do a little bit of sightseeing, as I had not done any since arriving.

With each new change came a reminder of how far I had come since leaving England. I felt as if a piece of my heart would always belong to Joe and I was pleased to have that distance between us, because I knew that it would be so easy to believe him when he claimed to be a changed person. My anxiety levels were much lower that they had been, but I was still hyper vigilant and would catch myself jumping at unfamiliar noises and feeling anxious whenever I had to meet new people. I had made a promise to myself when I got out of hospital, and I told myself that I would never let anxiety hold me back. I would instead see it as a challenge to battle through it, and so far I had done myself proud.

****

The following month Susan and I left for Brisbane. We had booked into a two-bedroom apartment at Kangaroo Point with views overlooking the Brisbane River. We arrived at seven pm on a Thursday night and I planned to view my new work place and a few apartments the following day.

We arrived at our apartment after a two-hour plus drive, thanks to city traffic. We were staying next to the Storey Bridge and there were several restaurants and bars and plenty of hustle and bustle. It felt strange after coming from the quiet property in Toowoomba and at first I felt a little overwhelmed by it. We found a quiet

Thai restaurant within the apartment complex and booked a table for an hour's time.

I was hoping to rent an apartment within walking distance of the office because I didn't want to buy a car unless I had to. We headed to the restaurant after enjoying a walk and ordered a glass of chilled white wine and we sat there for a few leisurely hours, enjoying the three courses and chatting about life in general. Susan told me all about her arrival in Australia thirty years ago. She explained how different everything was and how there were very few shops or restaurants. I tried to picture it in my head but I just couldn't imagine how desolate it must have been. We had a lovely evening and walked back to the apartment at ten o'clock with sleepy heads and full stomachs.

The following morning I walked to what would become my new office. It was still part occupied by whoever had been leasing it and they were busy moving furniture out when I arrived. They were very pleasant and allowed me to have a wander around to get a feel for the place. I was impressed at my office-to-be, which was very grand. It was situated at the rear of the large room and was big enough for a good sized desk, cabinets, a sofa and chairs. The glass was frosted so I had privacy, which was important because I would otherwise become distracted with what was happening outside in the main office. There were five desks, which were situated outside my office, with enough distance between the two to make that area feel completely separate. There was a space for an admin assistant at the entrance to the floor, directly opposite the lift, and a conference room big enough to seat at least sixteen people. I felt excited when I pictured myself here and couldn't wait to start. The nerves I had about moving to Brisbane suddenly diminished and I felt as if I had something to look forward to.

Next on my 'to do' list were the two apartments I had arranged to view. I wanted Susan to go with me, so we met up and had a coffee before walking to the first apartment, just three minutes away. This was a small and compact, one bedroom apartment with balcony. It wasn't very spacious, but then I didn't have a lot to put in it. The second apartment was bigger, but I felt that it was too big and it didn't feel as warm and safe as the first, so I asked to lease the smaller apartment starting in three weeks' time. That would give me the chance to look for some furniture and get settled before I started my new job.

I went out to lunch with Susan to celebrate what I hoped would be a smooth transition into my new job.

"I'm going to miss you, Charlotte. I've enjoyed having another woman around, especially a one who gets my sense of humour and understands me," she smiled. "And I will miss you. I can't ever thank you enough for everything that you have both done. I was broken when I arrived and you've helped heal me." I said.

"Are you ready to talk yet? Do you want to tell me what happened?" Susan asked gently.

I started talking and found it too difficult. A tidal wave of emotion hit me as the memories were released so I stopped. I wasn't ready to go back there and I didn't want to spoil my trip. "Sorry. Not yet. I just can't." "Plenty time, my darling. Plenty time," Susan said as she rubbed my arm.

We finished our drinks and went to get changed. Susan wanted to show me Southbank.

Southbank was a tourist attraction unlike anything I'd ever seen before. Bang in the middle of the city, there was a man-made beach and huge lagoon style swimming pool that was surrounded by lush gardens and numerous restaurants and fast food outlets, and the Brisbane Eye was also within walking distance. We spent the afternoon relaxing by the pool and swimming before rounding off the day with a meal. The view was breathtaking and made me feel even more excited about moving here.

The following day we spent the morning at the koala sanctuary and I could have happily stayed there all day. We saw dingoes, wombats and crocodiles. There were emus walking gracefully through the park, pecking randomly every now and then with their enormous beaks, while wallabies and kangaroos hopped around the enclosure in the hope of more food.

After having photographs taken with a koala and an enormous python, we hopped into a taxi into the bustling city centre. There were people everywhere: street carts, restaurants and bars in the middle of the street. The place was alive and vibrant and I loved it, and everyone seemed to be relaxed. There were street artists entertaining people and an aboriginal man dressed in cultural cloth and body paint, playing the didgeridoo.

We went into the enormous David Jones shopping centre and I bought myself some new make-up and clothes for work. After all, I was going to be in a managerial position so I had to make a good impression. We walked and shopped until we were exhausted and then went back to the apartment with some take out sushi.

The following morning we packed the car and headed out of the city, back to Toowoomba. I had a feeling that I was going to love living in Brisbane.

CHAPTER 13

Weeks turned into months and before I knew it I had been living in Brisbane for almost one year. I was relishing the challenge of my new position. My apartment was a short walk from my office, which worked really well for me and I was now a regular at the local Italian and called there two nights a week for fresh pasta take out, to save me cooking.

I liked my compact apartment, but I seemed to spend more time in my office than at home and if truth be known, I preferred that because a busy mind was far better than an idle mind in my opinion. If I sat around doing nothing, I started to think of the past and I knew that I needed to stay focused on the present and future.

Once a month I drove the ninety minute plus journey to spend a night with Susan and Will. I took them treats from the local delicatessen that they couldn't get in Toowoomba: homemade ginger and orange marmalades, pâté, infused oils and handmade chocolates. It was my way of saying thank you for everything that they had done for me when I had first arrived.

My twenty first birthday was only a few weeks away and Susan and Will wanted to go to Fraser Island for two nights to celebrate. We booked a two-bedroom apartment overlooking the sea. I was looking forward to a weekend away from work. As much as I enjoyed what I did, I was also aware that I became unhealthily obsessed with my job and time out would be good for me.

I received the best birthday news from my solicitor the day before we left. The house that Joe and I had bought was now sold. I felt as if another weight had been lifted off my shoulders and I was another step closer to closure. The money would be transferred into my bank account within a few days and I felt the noose around my neck slacken. I would be glad when the divorce came through so that I could cut the noose altogether and move on with my life.

Susan, Will and I enjoyed a relaxing weekend, walking, swimming and kayaking. We ate far too much and drank far too much but that was half the fun of it and we promised each other that we would do it again in the New Year.

****

Work was great and the business was doing really well but I was feeling a little awkward because I had an admirer. His name was Gregg and he was one of the directors. He was six foot one inch (approximately) and well built. You could tell that he looked after himself the way his clothes clung to his body. He had blonde, floppy hair that kind of did its own thing and despite always being dressed immaculately in a suit and crisp white shirt, I always pictured him in board shorts with a surf board under his arm. We met every four weeks, and the board consisted of five members, three men: Bob, my boss, Gregg, and Adam; and two women, Janelle and Renae. Gregg had started off very businesslike when I first met him; commending me on the great job I was doing and asking my opinion on how best to take the company forward. I came up with the idea of offering discounts for long-term lease clients and I proposed that we host an open day promotion with champagne and aperitifs. I suggested sending out invites to all the local mining and industrial firms and then enticing them in with a bonus: fifteen percent off first hire plus additional incentives. Gregg was impressed. I had sourced some information that gave us an idea of who the big companies were leasing from, as well as what they were paying and I suggested undercutting. It's amazing what you can find out when you call a firm, claiming that you've lost an invoice and need to complete the paperwork because you are new to the office.

"Above board but sneaky, I like it,' Gregg had said with a glint in his eye.

I preferred to think of it as productive and resourceful.

After leaving the room following one of our board meetings, Gregg followed me out. "So where is your office, Charlotte?"

"Follow me and I'll show you," I said, feeling uncertain all of a sudden.

"Nice," he said as he scanned my hand, obviously looking for a ring and signs of commitment. "So how long have you been in Australia and what brought you here?' He smiled with a hint of something: I wasn't sure quite what it was: Flirting? Curiosity? Who knew? I was a bit out of practice and I wasn't exactly experienced when it came to men and boyfriends, but his personal questions threw me off guard. I could cope with work related inquisitions but not questions about my personal life. I liked to keep that private. "I have relatives here and I moved here almost two years ago," I replied aloofly. I knew I was being a little rude but I couldn't help myself. "And did you come alone or -?" The question hung in the air. "I notice you aren't wearing a ring so I'm assuming that you are not married."

Wow, this was getting more awkward by the minute. I could feel nerves settle in my chest and my breathing suddenly became strained. I could feel my face flush and I felt angry with myself. What on earth was I nervous about, for goodness' sake, he was only talking to me and yet, it was as if a switch had gone off inside me and gone was the self-controlled, focused manager, and hello, nervous young woman. "You assume right, but I fail to see how that is relevant in any way," I retorted.

"Sorry. That was rude of me." Gregg replied.

I saw the hint of a smile on the corner of his mouth. He had a full mouth and his lips looked soft. Immediately I felt myself flush red and I turned away to hide my embarrassment. "Could I make it up to you by taking you out to dinner on Saturday night?" he asked.

Usually I never mixed business with pleasure, but then again I had never been a manager in the position of being asked out by a board member. What if I said no and then he took a dislike to me? What if the opposite happened? Maybe I was over thinking. "I'd like to talk more about the business ideas you have," he said, trying to redeem himself. "I could book a table at the steak house around the corner. No strings."

"OK, I'll meet you there at seven thirty but I must get on, I have a lot to do."

I felt a mixture of excitement and anxiety at the thought of just agreeing to a date, even if it was a business one.

Saturday came and I felt unbelievably nervous. I couldn't decide what to wear and I tried on at least six different outfits: I felt that they were either too formal or too dressy.

I settled for a pair of fitted jeans, a black camisole and a black jacket. I put my small diamond studs in, squirted myself with Coco and headed out of the door.

Gregg was waiting for me outside when I arrived. "Wow, you look even better dressed down that you do dressed up."

"Thank you," I said shyly, blushing at the compliment. It was a long time since I had felt that heady rush from a simple comment.

The hours flew by and despite my initial hesitance and nerves, I really relaxed and enjoyed Gregg's company. We talked easily from everything about the economy to places we would like to travel to. Gregg told me that he was twenty-seven and had never been married, but he had been in a long term relationship which had ended two years ago. He had known Bob, the owner of BRB, for years and had thought that the expansion of his business was a sound investment, so he had invested some money in the company in exchange for a percentage of the profits. He was considering increasing his share.

We left the restaurant just after eleven o'clock. "I'll walk you to your apartment. Which way is it?" he asked is that sexy Australian accent. "There's no need, Gregg, it's only a five minute walk from here and it's perfectly safe."

"No, I insist. You can't be too sure at this time of night."

We walked side by side and arrived at the entrance to my apartment block. "Thank you for a delightful evening, Charlotte. Your accent is almost as charming as you.' He smiled and I found myself drawn in to his brown eyes.

He kissed me on the cheek and asked if it would be OK to give me a call but did not expand on when that would be. Nor did he try to kiss me on the mouth with those soft lips of his. I was charmingly surprised and just a tiny bit offended.

I sat on the balcony drinking coffee and playing over the events of the night in my head. Gregg was handsome, smart, and funny and he appeared to be genuine. However, as much as he appealed to me I just could not let myself relax and go with the flow. Already my instincts were telling me to stay away and not get involved. My inner voice was asking, *What if he's another Joe?*

It's so hard to move forward and trust people after you've been hurt. You become suspicious and your vision of the world is skewed. I hated that Joe had taken all the joy out of relationships for me. When you invest that much love in someone, only for that person to destroy you, it changes your view on the world and how it works. Your innocence is gone forever because you can never allow yourself to enter that fairy tale love bubble again.

And so a pattern was set. Gregg would call me every week without fail and occasionally he popped into the office, feigning that he needed to collect some paperwork, but maybe he thought that the one on one approach would work better. Sometimes I let him take me out and other times I made excuses. The problem was I liked him and I wasn't quite sure how to handle that.

We kept that routine that for almost a year and he never complained or demanded more. I talked to Susan about it the next time I went to Toowoomba.

"Charlotte, I know you have been to hell and back with Joe, but please don't let that awful man ruin the rest of your life. Gregg sounds like a lovely young man from what you have said and you're too young. You have to live a little and enjoy yourself. You once told me that you saw anxiety as a challenge. Well, why not see this as one of the challenges that you need to overcome? Go out with him, my darling, and be happy. You deserve it more than anyone that I know."

I thought about Susan's words all of the way home. I knew she was right so I did something that I had never done before. I texted Gregg and I asked him if he would like to come around to my apartment for a meal and stay overnight. The butterflies in my stomach reminded me that not everything had been destroyed by Joe. I felt as if I was making a small commitment, but I also felt that I needed to be up front with Gregg.

When I got home I spent an hour prepping a lasagne and then I got showered, dressed and put a little make-up on.

I felt excited to see him and impressed that I had allowed myself to go with that, rather than fight it.

After we had finished our meal I looked at Gregg and took a deep breath before speaking.

"I feel that I owe you an explanation, Gregg. You must feel as if I am playing hard to get and wondering what it's all about. I'm not playing games at all and I need you to know that. I just find it a struggle at times with ghosts from the past. I used to be married and you are the first man that I have spent time with since that marriage ended. I don't want to go into details but I was abused by my husband, and the impact it had on me was huge. I can't commit to anything at the moment. All I can do is promise that I will try to let my guard down but you will need to be patient. If it feels as if I have too much baggage, I completely understand." I felt really proud of myself for talking about my feelings and it felt so much better now that I had laid my cards on the table. "Charlotte, I'm not stupid. I knew something had happened to you because you don't let anyone in to your private world. I was surprised when you invited me here tonight. Surprised and happy I might add. I love spending time with you. You intrigue me and I want to get to know more about you. We'll move as quickly or as slowly as you want and if I come on too strong, just tell me to back off." I smiled and for the first time since I'd laid eyes on Gregg, I felt as if there may be hope for a future between us.

****

After almost three years of being at BRB I was offered the position as Chief Executive Officer. If I accepted the post I would be offered a significant pay rise, as well as company perks such as a car, travel expenses, bonus potential and more. Bob wanted to take more of a back seat and spend time with his wife. She had been to Brisbane a few times but she had been born and bred in Toowoomba and wanted to stay there. Bob said that he trusted me to take over the business in Brisbane. I spent the weekend thinking about it, and after discussing it with Gregg I decided to accept the offer.

Gregg and I were still together but I was strict about how much time I spent with him. I let him stay over two nights a week and that was all. I was still afraid to give in and commit fully to the relationship, but Gregg was understanding and very patient. After what I had been through I needed some control and I was in no hurry to speed things ups anytime soon.

I took over as CEO seven weeks later. To be honest there was not much difference to my role other than that if anything went wrong, it was completely down to me and I would not have Bob there to seek guidance from, but I knew that I could call him if I needed to. I enjoyed my new role and time flew by in a blur of work and time spent with Gregg and Susan and Will.

I received my decree nisi via post a few weeks later and was officially a free woman. I still carried some sadness at what could have been, but my life was moving on from the horror of the past and I was finally able to look to the future, a future without Joe.

I became an Australian resident on May the first, after being in Australia for four years. I celebrated by inviting Susan and Will to Brisbane for the weekend. I booked them into a hotel not far from where I lived and told them that it was an early Christmas present. This would be the first time that Gregg had met my family. They hit it off from the word go and we had a marvellous day with a celebratory dinner on board the *Kookaburra* paddleboat. We ate delicious food and drank champagne while laughing about my early days in Toowoomba.

I had come a long way.

CHAPTER 14

A few months passed by and everything was going great. The business was doing well and profits were up by fifteen percent. I thought that I was finally living the life that I deserved to and that nothing could touch me.

That is, until *he* walked back into my life and straight into my office one day, and turned my whole world upside down. Joe had tracked me down in Australia and I had fled in panic.

I was sat in my office and Jess buzzed through to tell me that Mr Johnstone had arrived. I was intrigued to meet this elusive character because he had been extremely vague about which company he worked for, but he had assured Jess that he could bring a lot of business our way. He had asked for me specifically and although this was not unusual because of the networking I did, potential clients usually gave up some information about the company they owned or worked for.

I heard the door open and Jess usher him in before closing the door after her. I lifted my head from my desk and came eye to eye with Joe. He was dressed in a grey suit and pink shirt.

"Well, hello, Char-lotte,' he said separating my name deliberately. "You certainly have come a long way since I last saw you. Did you really think you could walk away from me without a backward glance? Did you think I would let you take our house and marriage without a fight? I told you that you were mine."

He started walking around the office, touching things. My head was spinning and I could feel my whole body drain as adrenalin surged through my blood at top speed. I couldn't speak or think and I felt as if I was going to choke if I stayed in the room one minute longer. I grabbed my bag and ran out of the office. I could hear alarmed shouts after me as I spun around to see where Joe was.

He stood in the doorway, shrugging his shoulders as if he had no idea what was going on and then he glared at me in the eye and I saw through into the evil that lay behind them. It all happened in seconds but it was enough for me to know that I needed to get away.

****

I turned and looked at Margie.

"And that is how I ended up here in Cairns."

"That's some story there, young lady. You must be a very strong woman and you should be proud of yourself for what you've been through. What will you do now?" "I have to go back and speak to my boss. My phone has been going crazy and the hardest part of it is that most of what I've just told you, I've kept secret. I was embarrassed and didn't want people to know about it, so I said nothing. I have a lot of explaining to do, especially to Gregg. Now come and let me walk you back to your hotel, it's almost daylight."

I hugged Margie and thanked her for listening to my story for the past six hours. "The pleasure was all mine, Charlotte. I hope that bastard has gone as far away from here as possible and I wish you all the best for your future. If you're ever in the Beaufort area, just ask where I live and someone will point you in my direction."

With that Margie walked off into her hotel and I went to mine. I lay on the bed and fell into a deep sleep, waking just after three pm. I showered and popped out for a pizza and then I called Gregg. "Charlotte. What the fuck is going on? I have been out of my mind. Why did you take off like that? I was on the verge of calling the police."

"I'm sorry, Gregg, I panicked and just needed to get away. There's a lot I need to tell you about my ex-husband and I feel bad that I've put you through all of that worry. Can you come around to my apartment tomorrow night when you finish work and I'll explain everything?"

"Where are you, and I'll come and get you now?" "I'm in Cairns. I've booked a hotel in Townsville and I'm driving there soon. I'll stay overnight and then I'll drive back to Brisi early the following morning. If I leave at five am I should be back for around eight. I'll call you when I'm home and we can talk if it's not too late."

"As long as you promise never to put me through anything like this again. I'll see you tomorrow. Drive safely. I love you, Charlotte." "You, too," I replied before ending the call. I was aware that every part of me held back from showing my feelings. I wanted to cry to Gregg and tell him that I needed his arms around me and that I loved him too, but instead I held him at arm's length.

I was dreading going back to Brisbane and hoped that Joe had disappeared and returned back home to the UK.

I jumped in the car and headed back down south to face the music and confront my past. I still hadn't decided how to handle Joe, but I had plenty of thinking time ahead of me over the twenty-four hours.

****

Gregg was waiting outside my apartment when I arrived. I was stiff and aching from being inside the car for almost fourteen hours. I had only stopped for toilet breaks and wanted nothing more than a hot bath and my bed. I regretted asking him to meet me here now. He looked annoyed and I was too tired to deal with any upset.

I spent the next few hours skimming and summarising my life story as best I could, so that he could get an understanding of my reaction when Joe had turned up.

"I'll fucking kill the son of a bitch of I catch him anywhere near you."

"No, Gregg. That is exactly what he wants. He would love to see you arrested and lose your job. He's not the kind of person you can reason with. You have to leave me to sort this out. I am speaking to Bob tomorrow, but I have decided that I need to take some time off work - I'm well overdue a holiday and I need to put some distance between myself and this place for another week or two. Hopefully he will fly back home soon. He'll get fed up with looking for me and if he does stay around, I'll go to the police."

"OK, whatever you want, babe. I think I should move in here in the meantime, to make sure you're safe." "I won't let Joe rule my life, Gregg. You can stay until I go on holiday if you want and then, well, let's just see."

I heard Gregg sigh as I walked away. He was so patient, always asking me to move in with him or vice versa and asking me to marry him. He had put up with the rejection so far, but who knew how long for.

The following morning I sat in the office with Bob. He had travelled from Toowoomba when I took off and I was grateful that he had not told Susan and Will about the incident with Joe. I knew that they would worry and there was really nothing they could do so it was best that they didn't know. "You need to talk to me and tell me what's happening for you at the minute, Charlotte,' he said, looking concerned. 'In the years that you have worked here I have never known you take one day off sick, let alone disappear for four days. You have not returned messages and frankly, it is so out of character that I am left floundering. I almost called the police, for God's sake. Are you ill?"

I sat feeling nervous, which was out of character for me with Bob, but familiar in connection to my past. I twisted my hands and took a deep breath.

"Bob, all I can do is apologise. I know that it was out of character but I was in shock, I guess. It will take a while for me to explain what happened in my past and how that past has come knocking on my door again, quite literally! I hope that once I've talked to you, you will understand why I reacted the way I did."

And so I began at the beginning. I told him all about the early days of the relationship, the proposal and then the wedding. Then I told him about the death of my parents and the start of the controlling behaviour which led to violence and finally the miscarriage and breakdown. In a strange way it felt a relief to let it all out after such a long time. I no longer needed to hide from my past now, I could finally be at peace with who I was.

It's strange how, despite knowing it was Joe's wrong doing, I still felt a degree of shame and found it easier not talking about it. Almost fearful, I guess, of being judged by others. People who have not experienced domestic violence think that it is as easy as picking up a bag and walking out. They don't see that there is a progressive cycle that is followed, that it is not all bad at first - that despite their behaviour and projection on to you, you still love them. They isolate you to make sure that there is no one else in your life able to see what is happening. You are quite literally alone with your lover/perpetrator, being constantly told that you are crazy, impossible to live with, ugly, too fat/thin etc. ... Leaving is the most vulnerable time for a woman because the abusers feels that they have lost control and this can escalate their behaviour: so, contrary to what people think, it actually takes an enormous amount of courage to walk away.

I looked at Bob, who had gone very quiet.

"It took me years to accept what happened. Having a nervous breakdown is not something to be proud of but I had been through so much and Joe just pushed me over the edge with his abuse. At first I believed him. I believed that it was all my fault. It wasn't until I saw a psychologist that she was able to identify the cycle of domestic violence and I saw for the first time that I wasn't crazy, that I wasn't selfish or a bitch. I saw the truth. I saw that he was a manipulating, controlling and violent man who was unwilling to take responsibility for his behaviour. That was when I knew I needed to get away from him. I knew he would never leave me alone if I stayed there and quite honestly, after all of my loss I felt that I had nothing left to stay for. I came here to stay initially for a holiday, to get my strength back. I loved the freedom that I had here. I loved that I didn't feel as anxious, and for the first time in years I could talk to people without being judged - and most importantly, I loved that people *wanted* to talk to me. When your self-esteem is at rock bottom you tend not to say much to people. You feel as if you have nothing worth saying.

In time I found my voice and my confidence grew and that's down to you offering me the job and believing in me. I never talked about it because I worried that you would judge me and think me incapable of doing the job. People have preconceived ideas when it comes to mental health."

Bob looked overwhelmed by what I had told him.

"OK. I need some time to absorb this Charlotte. I appreciate your honestly and just wish that you had felt able to disclose this earlier on, but thank you for sharing that. I am still confused as to why you took off that day, though."

I stood up and looked out of his window. It was one of the most stunning views of the city I had seen. I loved this city but now it felt as if the sparkle had dimmed, I would no longer feel safe enough to wander the streets on a day off, exploring back street shops, or grab a coffee and sit in the mall, people watching.

"Looking back, I guess there were a few indicators that something wasn't right. Libby had taken a call from a Mr Johnston, who had stated that he wanted to meet with me specifically. He was reluctant to give a company name because he said he was in the process of taking over a large company and there would be a name change. Mr Johnstone turned out to be Joe. He walked into my office as brazen as brass. I still can't believe it. He's so unpredictable and who knows what he is capable of. All of the fear from the past came crashing in around me and I just needed to get away. There's no reasoning with him. He used to tell me if I left that he would kill me or get someone else to kill me, and there's a part of me that feels as if I am on borrowed time. I panicked. I'm so sorry. I know my behaviour was unprofessional and now that you know about it, I just hope it won't affect my position here."

Bob grabbed my hand. "Charlotte, you are by far the best CEO I could wish for. There is no way we want to lose you, so stop worrying. What we need to do is think how we can keep you safe, both at work and at home. How about we get something to eat and that will give me time to think, and then we'll talk about what to do from there."

So we headed out for a sushi lunch. Bob took a few calls and we walked back along the river. He sat down on one of the wooden benches that overlooked the river and patted the seat next to him. We sat in silence for a few minutes, watching the ripples of the water and the people standing on the wharf, waiting on the next ferry.

The sun glistened on the water and beamed down upon us. It had become such a familiar feeling and always made me feel happy inside; that is, until the sun hid behind a cloud and everything darkened. I felt as if *I* had a big black cloud hanging over me and I feared that Joe was behind it.

Bob was sitting forward with his hands clasped. He sighed as he looked at me.

"I've been thinking briefly Charlotte, and I think it would be a good idea if you took a holiday. That will give you time to unwind and relax, which I feel is important after what has happened recently. Don't look alarmed: your job is safe. I guarantee that. In fact it is non-negotiable. I have allowed you to work far too long without a break and that was wrong of me. Book a holiday somewhere and take four weeks' leave. You can spend the rest of this week going through bookings etc. and pass some of that responsibility on to Tess; that is what she's paid for. I have also instructed security to keep an eye out for your ex-husband and we have identified him via security cameras, so both men know what he looks like. I can assure you he won't be allowed back in the building. Regarding your safety outside of work, I spoke to my friend who is in the police force and he suggested popping into the station and discussing the possibility of taking out a domestic violence order. That would stop him coming to your home or bothering you and would maybe make you feel as if you have some control over this."

I sat quiet for a moment and then nodded. "Oh, I know all about domestic violence orders because the police took one out against him in England."

I sat quiet for a moment and allowed his words to sink in.

"OK the holiday is a done deal, I was going to ask you for time off anyway, I need to put some distance between myself and Joe," I said, smiling. "It might actually be nice to take some time out after what's just happened."

I left Bob and headed to the travel agent and came out with an armful of brochures. I spent the evening going through the brochures with Gregg, but could not decide between Kenya, which had a mix of activity and relaxation, or a cruise around the Pacific islands. I wished that Gregg was going with me but at such short notice, he couldn't take time off from work, and maybe it was for the best, as it would give me time to get my head together.

After a night of restless sleep I decided upon a cruise.

I liked the idea of getting on and off different islands and exploring, and I felt as if I could get lost on a ship. If I wanted to be social I could be, but I also had a choice, which meant that there was no pressure on me to participate in anything unless I wanted to. There were numerous activities and swimming pools on board, as well as a casino, three spas, shops, and an array of restaurants to choose from.

I was booked to leave in four days' time, and the first three days would be spent at sea, and on the fourth the ship would dock at New Caledonia. I would have eight hours to explore the island before boarding again. On the fifth day the ship would dock at an island in Vanuatu, and the following day we would be out at sea. The remainder of the cruise would be spent visiting two of the Fijian islands with the final destination being the Isle of Pines. In total the cruise lasted twelve days and I had splurged on a penthouse with veranda, which was costing me just under ten thousand dollars. I figured that as I hadn't had a holiday in years - I might as well enjoy the one I was having. This penthouse came with butler service and in-suite breakfast, lunch and dinner service, so if I didn't feel like eating with everyone else on board, I could eat in my room. The room looked fabulous and spacious and I would also be able to take my laptop and do a bit of work. There was a movie room, in-house entertainment, security cameras, and a veranda outside of the master suite complete with seating.

I packed a mixture of clothing, from casual to elegant and formal. I was unsure what the dress code would be so I wanted to make sure I going to fit in, and what woman doesn't enjoy having plenty of outfits to choose from?

Gregg dropped me off at the dock and I felt strangely excited as well as a touch nervous. This would be the first time that I had holidayed alone. I loved the anticipation of what I would find on board and the thought of exploring the different islands filled me with a sense of delight. It would be the perfect tonic after my recent shock.

I was one of the first to board, perks of booking the penthouse, and I was taken personally to my suite, where I was introduced to the waiter and told to ask for whatever I wanted. I felt a bit of a fraud if I'm honest, I had no intention of ordering a waiter around: I had simply chosen this suite because it gave me fabulous views, and was the most spacious yet private suite.

I unpacked my cases while the other guests boarded, and spent time looking around my suite. There was a sofa and three single chairs in the lounge area, a dining table and soft chairs in the adjoining dining area. The bedroom had a king size bed with soft chairs and patio doors leading onto the veranda, and an ensuite fit for a king. There was a small cinema room and a bar full of every drink imaginable.

Once all of the guests had boarded, which took quite some time, we pulled out of dock and I decided to have a walk around the ship to get my bearings.

There were twelve decks in total and each deck had their own bar, pool and eating areas. Deck seven was the entertainment deck and it included a celebrity theatre that boasted Broadway style shows, a club, bar, shops, a ballroom and a casino. There were outdoor heated swimming pools and spas and entertainment areas for children as well as quiet relaxing areas for adults.

I rang Bob to tell him that I had boarded the ship and was officially on my holidays but the reception was patchy and I wasn't sure if he had heard me. I opened my emails and found out that Joe had turned up at the office two days ago and he had created a bit of fuss, so security had called the police. He had managed to get into the building under the guise of a repair man and he had made it up to the seventh floor, where my office was. He spoke Monica on reception and then she realized that something was up when he insisted that I had called him. Thankfully I had been on leave: otherwise, chances are he would have been shown into my office. Again! I shivered as I thought of his persistence. Everyone had received a memo from Bob and thankfully Jessica had called security. I felt my stomach churn as I thought about him taking such extreme measures but then decided to worry about that *after* my holiday.

I ate a leisurely lunch and read a few chapters of the book that I had picked up in one of the shops. I had decided that I would eat dinner at six and then go and watch a theatre production of *Grease*, one of my favourite movies.

I requested my meal in my room because I still felt a little strange about eating amongst couples and families while alone. Once I had familiarized myself with the ship, I would be able to decide where I felt most comfortable to dine alone.

I finished my meal and opted for a knee length fitted dress and sandals, I put my diamond studs in, and I tied my hair up, allowing a few tendrils to hang lose creating a relaxed but sophisticated look.

I took the elevator to the theatre and I was pleased to see that it was fairly empty when I arrived, so I sat in the middle row, third from the front.

After about fifteen minutes a few people started to stream in and apart from a row of four to the very front of me, there was no one around me and I liked that; it felt as if I had the theatre to myself.

I was engrossed in the start of the production, the part where Sandi is at school and the girls are being mean to her, when I felt someone sit down next to me. I could feel myself internally tut with annoyance. There were hundreds of empty seats, why next to me? Out of annoyance I refused to look at them and instead focused on the show. It was up to the part where the boys were getting ready to race their cars and Sandy was not far off her sexy transformation.

"I'd still love to see you in that outfit again," the voice next to me said. I froze inside and felt my skin prickle. My breath stuck inside my chest, unable to escape with fear. I knew it was Joe before I looked at him. My mind started racing as to how he had found me. Almost as if he could read my mind he said, "You really need to employ more intelligent staff, Charlotte. All it took was a pair of overalls and a fake conversation for the giggly blonde receptionist to reveal that you were off on holiday on a well-deserved cruise around the Pacific islands. A few phone calls to the local cruise companies about a luggage query and bingo. Didn't manage to quite track down which floor or room you are in, but looks like I've found you anyway."

I looked at him out of the corner of my eye and saw him smirking, clearly proud of his efforts and ability to track me down.

Joe's reference to the outfit of tight black pants and off the shoulder top took me back to the night we had attended a fancy dress party. I had dressed up as Sandy and Joe had not been able to keep his hands or eyes off me. Of course, that was in between him accusing me of looking at almost every man in the room. When we got home we had sex several times. He told me that no one would ever be able to satisfy me the way he could and that I would never experience sex like this with anyone else. I felt sick to the stomach that he would bring up such an intimate part of our relationship after everything that he had done.

I sat silent, trying to figure out how best to respond to him. I could try the calm, nice approach and hope to reason with him, but he might read into that and get his hopes up that we could reconcile. Given the lengths he had gone to I assumed that's what he wanted.

I could avoid him and refuse to speak, but that might anger him more. I felt that whatever I did would have an outcome one way or the other so I decided on the calm nice approach in the hope that he would remain calm enough for me to get away from him.

"What do you want, Joe? Why are you here?" I whispered.

"Well, we never had a chance to talk because you fucked off, so I've had to resort to tracking you down," he spat.

"We're divorced now, Joe, get over it!"

"You know for a fact that we were meant to be together. You fucked me up when you left. I know you still love me, Char. You always will. Remember our wedding day? We made a vow to stay together forever."

I turned to look at him and was shocked at the physical reaction I had when I saw him. My heart lurched in my chest and for split seconds distant memories, good memories, flooded through my mind and warmed me inside. I hated myself. He was so damn good looking and he knew it. I think it was his confidence that people noticed first, though. Never shy, always full of himself, it somehow gave him an air of authority. Despite his looks, though, I knew that he was the prime example of the saying, 'beauty is only skin deep'. He was nasty and selfish and never took responsibility for anything. He loved to blame other people for his mistakes and behaviour. He was violent and aggressive and abusive and a complete control freak.

Looking him straight in the eye I quietly spoke. "Nowhere in my wedding vows do I remember agreeing to be used as a punch bag."

I stood up and walked out of the theatre with my head held high. I was too scared to see if he was following me so I stared straight ahead. My heart was hammering in my chest, with the reality of the situation starting to hit me. I could feel myself shaking and I cursed myself for not bringing an emergency stash of diazepam. I was trapped on a ship with my abusive ex-husband for eleven days. I needed to find a way to get off.

****

I managed to make it back to my suite without being followed, I hoped. I asked the butler to bring me a mojito and not to let anyone else into my suite. He looked at me like I was crazy. I knew he finished work at eleven pm so I had two hours left to think of a way to solve this hideous situation. The ship was huge, so the chances of Joe finding me were slim but the longer I remained on board, the more at risk I would be. Thank God for security cameras.

I drank enough mojitos to get me drunk enough to help me fall asleep quickly. I could not believe that I was living this nightmare again. I had tried calling Bob and Gregg, but could not get a reception on my mobile. That left me feeling even more isolated and alone.

I woke up in the middle of the night suddenly. The only sound I could hear was the sound of the ocean outside. The ship rocked gently, which I found soothing as opposed to uncomfortable, but my luxurious suite now felt too big. I started imagining Joe hiding behind the plush gold curtains in the living area, or standing out on the balcony, waiting for me to open the door. I spent the rest of the night lying awake, trying to figure out what to do. I decided to try calling Gregg again in the morning.

I woke up at five am after the most frightful sleep. I showered and dressed and waited until the butler started at six am before asking him if he could bring me some breakfast up. He arrived back after fifteen minutes and laid out a mini banquet of fruit and yoghurt, fresh juice, toast, croissants and jam and a cooked breakfast of eggs, bacon, mushroom, sausage, beans and tomato. I thanked him and excused him. I sat on the veranda picking at the fruit. My appetite had gone. I could not think of a worse situation to be in. I sat there trying to get a connection on my phone for what seemed like eternity, and then headed to the door to let the butler back in who was most likely back to collect the breakfast dishes.

I opened the door and was pushed aside by Joe, who then closed and locked the door behind him. He grabbed me, pushing up against the wall with his hand squeezing around my neck. Adrenalin pulsed through my veins like ice, inhibiting my ability to think rationally and squeezing air out of my lungs like a compressor.

"Think you're above me, bitch? Think you can just walk away again like you did years ago? Well, guess what? You're fucking wrong!"

He slammed my head against the wall.

I drifted in and out of consciousness for who knows how long: seconds, minutes, hours. I had no idea.

I came to and he was sat on the bed. He looked dishevelled. He had a glass of whiskey in his hand and a bottle of Jameson stood on the bar top with two thirds missing. I guessed he had been drinking all night and I knew that this was when he was at his most dangerous, and at that moment I cursed the extensive and very lavish free bar in my room. He ran his fingers through his hair, picked the bottle of whiskey up and looked at me.

"You see, Char," he said as he waved the bottle drunkenly, sloshing it on the plush cream carpet. "This is what you do to me. You make me do these things because you are so fucking unreasonable. How hard is it to talk to someone? If you would stop running away from me I wouldn't have to teach you a lesson, would I? I wouldn't have to hunt you down like some kind of fucking animal, would I? You fuck my head up and then expect me to be reasonable."

His voice was getting louder and he was visibly becoming more and more agitated. I sat propped against the wall, fear crashing through me at a frightening speed. My mouth was bone dry and my head was pounding sending piercing splinters of pain into my skull, causing me to wince. I had a sense of detachment and felt as if I was watching the scene from another angle, almost like a bystander. There was a gnawing fear in the pit of my stomach that kept rearing up into my throat, knocking the breath out of me in sharp bursts. My chest was so tight and contracted that breathing no longer felt natural; it was forced and laboured. I thought about dying and I wondered if it would hurt. He was never going to stop; I knew that now. No matter what restrictions were put in place, no matter how many domestic violence orders I took out. It was partly my fault for not breaching him, but all I had wanted was to be left alone. I saw now that I'd underestimated him, I should have gone straight to the police and told them everything.

Joe stood up and started walking around the bedroom, waving the whiskey bottle as he went, and intermittently taking large gulps of it. I looked at him, wild eyed, frantic, with droplets of whiskey running down his face and I stayed silent.

His ranting came in waves not dissimilar to the sea we were sailing across.

"That fucking house that was supposed to be so perfect. Why would I want to stay there on my own and how the fuck could I afford it by myself? It was all part of your plan to ruin me."

"You sold your parents' house without even asking me if I minded. That's a bastard's trick."

The noise and ranting floated in and out as I waited. I waited for something. I knew that there was little I could do and the word 'death' hovered above me like a vulture waiting to pounce. I became more terrified the more Joe drank. Some of the worst beatings he had given me were from when he was drunk, so I knew he wouldn't go easy on me.

Suddenly he grabbed me by the collar and shoved me forward, faster than my feet could carry me. I ended up being dragged onto the balcony, where he staggered and then attempted to force me over the rail. It was almost like a cheesy scene from a movie, albeit an extremely horrific one. I pushed at him and fought with what strength I had to push him off me. He alternated between attempting to get me over the barrier and then threatening to take us both together. It all passed by in seconds but it felt like hours. I was screaming for all I was worth but I wasn't even sure if there was any sound coming out. At times I wasn't sure who it was pulling and grabbing, and I lost sense of all my surroundings. I gave one almighty push to free myself as we both hung part over the rail, and I watched. I watched as the man I had once loved tumbled down towards the ocean, grabbing at air with flailing arms and legs. He never took his eyes off me as I watched him. I heard the door flying open and staff rushed in. There was mayhem below as a life raft and ring were thrown from one of the lower decks. There was no way I could imagine Joe surviving a fall of approximately two hundred foot. The enormity of it all hit me and I passed out.

I came to in the medical centre and a doctor was standing next to me.

"Hi, Charlotte. I'm Doctor Paul Johnston. I gave you a shot of diazepam because of the shock and to help calm your nerves so you may feel a little groggy or detached from reality. How are you feeling?"

I felt numb and sick. Very sick. "Joe?" I asked, his name hanging in the sterile air. "What happened?"

"I'm very sorry to say Charlotte, that he did not make it. Joe is dead."

I lay there, stunned at what had just happened, trying to make sense of it all.

"I have spoken to the captain and despite the tragedy, the ship must continue on its course, but you are welcome to get a boat back to Brisbane when we dock at New Caledonia tomorrow.

"We have watched the security footage from your room and balcony. Mr Porter also assaulted the butler, knocking him unconscious and tying him up, it was only when shift change occurred that we found him, which is when we gained access into your room.

"There will be a ship docking on the return journey so we can arrange for you to board that one to Brisbane, and of course it goes without saying that you will get a partial refund for not completing the journey, under the circumstances."

I nodded and lay back closing my eyes, horrified at what had taken place but relived that it was finally over. I just wanted to get off this ship and go home to Gregg.

****

Gregg met me as I disembarked. I felt as if I had aged ten years in the past couple of days. He hugged me to him and for once I did not resist or fight him, I sank into his body and allowed myself to feel protected, and I let out all of the fear and anger that had built over the years.

"Charlotte. My god, I don't know what to say apart from thank God that bastard is dead. I'm sorry I feel like that but after I heard what had happened I thought about losing you and it scared the hell out of me."

"I am still in shock, Gregg, and I need to go to hospital to get checked out, I didn't realize that strangulation can cause problems days or even weeks after the incident. After that I need to go to the police station to make a statement. Could you get the footage of Joe turning up at work from one of the girls at work please? That would be really helpful in helping build a picture up, I will also hunt out my old DVO and all the paperwork relating to the assault from England. Hopefully all of the evidence together will be enough to show the police that this was not deliberate on my part."

Later that afternoon once I had been given the all clear from the hospital I went to the police station where I spent three hours explaining everything about my relationship with Joe: the violence in England, his arrest and threats to track me down, and Joe arriving in Australia and then turning up on-board the cruise ship.

The police watched the footage from work and from the cruise ship and informed me that they were satisfied that Joe had instigated the initial assault and that his death had been as a result of his own behaviour. Of course a coroner would need to confirm the cause of death, but they assured me that I would not be needed for further questioning.

The following day, after I had slept almost twelve hours and taken a long bath, I agreed to meet with Bob. I was bruised and felt battered physically as well as emotionally. I walked into the office and Monica rushed towards me.

"I am so sorry, Charlotte. I didn't know it was him and I told him that you were on holiday." She started crying. "It's fine, Monica. Joe was very good at getting what he wanted so if it hadn't of been you, it would have been someone else. Is Bob in the board room?"

"Yes. Sorry, again," she said as she dabbed at her eyes with a mascara stained tissue.

I walked into the board room and Bob came towards me with a bouquet of flowers that must have cost the equivalent of an average person's weekly wage.

I thanked him and sat down.

"I almost feel responsible for this, Charlotte, because I forced you to take a holiday. If you had been here -"

I put my hand up to stop him. "If I had of been here Bob, a similar scenario would have occurred. There was no stopping him, he was hell bent on having me, and if he couldn't, he was going to do his best to make sure nobody could. I hope you don't mind, but I've decided to go back to the UK on holiday. I owe it to Joe's parents to explain what happened and I have some friends that I need to reconnect with. Is that OK with you? I feel as if I have run away from my past for far too long and I need to make peace with it. On top of that, I wouldn't class this recent debacle as a holiday. At least I'll know I'll be safe this time. I'll take two months' leave. I want a few weeks here to rest and absorb what I've been through before I tackle the journey back."

"Of course, Charlotte. Whatever it takes to get you well and you know that I will support you through this. If there's anything I can do to help, just ask. Take as long as you need, we probably owe you five months' leave as it is. Keep in touch and please rest up until you've got your strength back. Oh, and let Gregg look after you."

I smiled at Bob. "I'll be fine. I can look after myself."

"There's no need to keep fighting now, Charlotte. The past has well and truly gone."

I closed my eyes and walked out of the office, towards the past that I had run away from for so long. I felt tears trickle down my face, mostly in relief that I was now truly safe, but also in grief for the man that I first fell in love with.

CHAPTER 15

I stepped off the plane at Newcastle Airport and the cold north-east English air took my breath away. I stopped and quietly absorbed the familiarity of home while I waited for my luggage. I can't quite explain the feeling of being surrounded by people who speak the same dialect as you. It's so comforting being surrounded by familiar sights, sounds and smells.

I walked outside and was saddened that there was no one there to greet me, and a wave of loneliness and grief washed over me. I imagined my parents standing there eager to see me, and my dad hugging me so tight that I would have to fight to get him off me. Death never fully leaves when you've lost a loved one, or in my case, loved *ones*. Still, I was home and I was looking forward to well and truly burying some ghosts from the past.

I was staying at a bed and breakfast that was central enough for me to visit my parents' grave and call in on the people that I wanted to see. I had arranged to see

Nicki while I was back and I was feeling very nervous about it after having cut her out of my life so abruptly all of those years ago, when I first moved to Australia. I really regretted doing that now.

I dumped my suitcase and bag in the room and took a walk along the river. It was cold and such a huge temperature drop for me, coming from the heat of Queensland. It was autumn and leaves had turned orange and brown as they lay scattered over roads and footpaths, blending in as if they had always been there. Trees were almost bare and sad looking and the sky was cloudy and dull, which added to the melancholy that I was feeling.

I was exhausted after the trip, but I also felt a fresh surge of energy with being home. It was cosy in the bed and breakfast and thankfully the owners didn't seem the type to want to know all about my life. They weren't local but once I told them that I was, they were happy to assume I didn't need any information on the area and they left me to do my own thing. I treat myself to fish and chips from the local fish and chip shop and found that after years of dreaming about them, I preferred Australian fish and chips. I had a chuckle to myself as recalled the number of times I had yearned after them.

Nicki was still living in Scotland, but she was catching a train and I was meeting her the next morning. I barely slept that night with excitement and nerves and I was up two hours before my alarm went off.

As soon as I saw her step off the train, I reverted back to being a teenager. I ran up and we squealed and hugged and cried and laughed, all at the same time. We headed to the park, where we knew we could talk without being overheard.

"Lotti, I have missed you so much, but I have to say Australia must suit you because you look amazing. I was heartbroken when I received your letter but I understand why you left. I still can't believe it all. What the hell happened on the cruise? You weren't making much sense when I spoke to you on the phone."

"I'm not sure where to start, Nicki, and I'm still coming to terms with Joe's death myself." I said, feeling sad.

We spent the rest of the day and evening filling in all of the gaps from years gone by. I apologised over and over to Nicki for not telling her where I was going and explained that I had tried to protect her. Even though Joe had never liked her, I knew that he would try and get information from Nicki, and he had proved me right. A few months prior to him turning up in Australia, Joe had harassed Nicki for information about where I was living. I still had no idea how he had tracked me down in Australia and I guessed I would never know the answer to that.

I had agreed to meet with Joe's parents the following day. I was dreading it because I had no idea what they did or didn't know about the separation and violence, let alone the events surrounding his death. His funeral had been four days ago and I assumed that it had been a quiet one because Nicki's brother had not known anything about it. I was beyond nervous as I pulled up to their house and memories that had been repressed started floating into my consciousness, making me emotional and shaky.

In total, I spent three hours with Joe's mum, mainly. His father left after forty minutes and I feared that the talk of the domestic violence was too much for him. Joe's mum was horrified at what I had been through and devastated that Joe had behaved like this. She did not go into detail about her relationship, but she did state that there had been some issues when Joe was young and maybe that had affected him.

I left and felt as though I had their blessing to move on with my life, and even though I had spent little time with them during the course of my relationship with Joe, I still felt relief that they knew the full picture.

When I left their house, I got in the car and drove to the graveyard. I walked towards Joe's gravestone and felt numb as I read his name etched into marble in gold. I then let the tears flow. All the tears that I thought were long gone came flooding out. The sorrow that things hadn't worked out between us, the pain of what I'd been through, the heartache I had felt when it was over, and the ongoing anxiety that I had lived with as a result of what he had put me through. I cried until I had no tears left and then I walked away from my past, determined to start living in the present, determined that I would no longer allow that man to destroy my future.

I called Gregg when I got back to the bed and breakfast.

"I'm so sorry for waking you. I know it's only five am in Oz but I needed to talk to you."

"Are you OK, Charlotte? What's so urgent?"

"Us. We are. I realised something, coming back here, Gregg. I've realised that it is time to let go of the past and starting living in the present. I've been so wrapped up in protecting myself that I've never really given you - well, us - a chance. Move in with me. Please."

I couldn't believe that I had put that out there because it felt like the biggest risk, but Gregg had been so patient, and I had been so afraid of being hurt again - but I'd finally realised that Gregg was not Joe and never would be, he was kind, loving and supportive. Joe had controlled my life when we were together and here I was, still allowing him to control my life years later. It was time to let go of the past. I deserved to be happy.

"Wow, that was unexpected and I must say, I was beginning to think it would never happen. Seeing as I am already here, I guess I'll just stay? Are you sure about this Charlotte?"

"I've never been more certain of anything in my life."

I telephoned Jimmy, dad's old friend and gave him a brief update on what had been happening. It was nice to hear his voice and we spent some time reminiscing about my parents. I also made contact with some of my older friends and girls I used to work with, and I explained that I'd been in a domestic violence relationship and that I'd not deliberately chosen to cut them out of my life. Some were more understanding than others and I accepted that after all of those years, those relationships would be unlikely to ever fully mend, but that was OK, I felt at peace with myself now.

I hugged Nicki as I stood near the boarding gate, ready to return to my life in sunny Australia. "Come with me, Nik. Book a holiday and I'll pay. You'll love it and now that you're a qualified hairdresser you can get work there without any problems, all you need to do is apply for a working holiday visa which will take about six weeks to come through, maybe even less."

Nicki laughed. "I'll think about it, babe, and I promise I will come and see you and Gregg soon. Love you."

I kissed her on the cheek and mouthed, "Love you too" as I walked into the departure lounge towards my new life, my life that would be free of fear because my walls of protection were finally crumbling.

****

Living with Gregg was a lot easier than I thought it would be. We laughed and enjoyed dining out, having a few close friends around for dinner on a weekend and sharing work thoughts and ideas.

We had agreed to buy a bigger apartment together and had been looking, but as of yet nothing had stood out for us, so for now we were cosy in my one bedroom apartment, which was struggling to hold all of our clothes and belongings.

Gregg proposed for the hundredth time one Friday evening. We had finished eating and we were snuggled up on the couch, enjoying a glass of wine while we browsed through the TV channels, looking for something worth watching.

"Marry me, Charlotte. I've asked you before and I won't stop asking you. You know I love you, so put me out of my misery. Please."

I kissed him on the lips tenderly before looking him in the eye.

"Ok," I smiled.

The look of shock on his face was priceless. He grabbed me and spun me around, knocking my glass of wine over in the process.

"You've said it now so no going back, tomorrow we're heading to the jewellers to buy a ring and then we're driving to Toowoomba to tell your aunt and uncle.

And the following day we did just that. We went into the city centre to choose a ring together. I wanted a Canadian square cut diamond and I found one that was the perfect in every way, understated but classy and elegant.

I rang Nicki to tell her the good news and Gregg rang his best mate. They laughed at how many times Gregg had told Brent that I'd turned him down and Brent would just shake his head and tell him to play it cool.

We drove out to see Susan and Will and we drank a glass of champagne on the veranda while watching the sun go down and it hit me, not for the first time, how truly blessed I was.

Gregg and I spent the next few months planning where to marry and who to invite to the wedding. I wanted an intimate wedding and Gregg agreed that minimal fuss was definitely the better option.

We had decided on a guest list of Susan and Will, Bob and his wife, and we would pay for Nicki to fly here. Gregg wanted his parents, Jan and Colin and his best mate, Brent. We would get married on one of the Whitsunday Islands and we would have a bigger party for work colleagues and friends when we returned to Brisbane.

We had found a Queenslander in one of the suburbs approximately eighteen kilometres out from Brisbane. It was perfect. It had four bedrooms, a wraparound veranda not dissimilar to Sue and Will's house, a big garden, and it was within walking distance of local shops and restaurants, so we put an offer in, which was accepted immediately.

I spoke to Nicki weekly now and we tried to Skype at least once every few weeks. I would send her pictures of the local attractions when we went out, so that she could get a feel for the place. It was an unspoken rule that she would be my bridesmaid again and this time I had her full blessing. She loved Gregg and chatted happily to him if I was busy with something, and the two of them got along famously. She had also agreed to come here for one year on a working holiday visa to see if she liked it. I was beyond excited at the thought of having her around and it would give us a chance to catch up on all of the years that we had missed out on.

****

Ten months later, we married on a beach on Daydream Island in the Whitsundays. I wore a white sleeveless full-length dress that was understated and elegant. The bodice area was gathered at the breast with a diamanté rose clasp and was nipped in at the waist. It fell in small folds of silk to my ankles and skimmed my figure, showing my curves. I wore flat sandals made of diamanté and carried a small posy of white arum lilies and purple lisianthus from Susan and Will's garden.

Gregg wore black trousers, a short sleeved white shirt, (because it was April and still quite hot): a waistcoat and a tie that almost matched the colour of the purple flowers in my posy, and Brent was almost identical, minus the waistcoat.

Gregg's parents had flown in from Armadale in Perth. This was the first time that I had met them in person, even though I had spoken to them on the telephone on numerous occasions. They were just as lovely as I thought they would be and they thanked me for making Gregg a very happy man. It was such a different experience from my first wedding because I already felt part of their family.

Will was dressed in an almost identical outfit to Gregg, and Susan wore a knee length cream dress with a purple flower in her hair.

Nicki looked stunning in a floor length purple dress and she wore white lilies in her hair.

I walked down the dark wood stairs, which were adorned with purple and white sashes and bows. The church was small, secluded, and situated on the beach and stood out against the dark wood decked area that it was mounted upon. There were lights around the entrance to the church and all of the shutter windows were open, allowing a tropical breeze to sift through while giving stunning views of the ocean. It was a small church with room for maybe a dozen people, but it was perfect and it was so intimate just the eight of us.

I had watched Brent's eyes light up as soon as he saw Nicki and I secretly hoped that the magic of the day would touch them two as well, after all they were both single!

We exchanged our vows inside the church and then stepped onto the beach where a small marquee had been set up, complete with champagne and canapés. We had asked for hot and cold food to be brought down at intervals, so we could relax and eat while talking and taking photographs.

There were easy chairs set up and a high set bar table and stools, all in the same matching design. There was a bar with a huge variety of drinks, a table with chilled champagne and wine and two bar staff to keep the drinks flowing. It was so carefree and relaxed and I could have happily stayed there forever.

Gregg beckoned me onto the sand in front of the church and then proceeded to roll his trousers up, scoop me into his arms and wade into the sea.

"What are you doing?" I laughed as he juggled me around, trying to get a firm grip. "Do not drop me in the water!"

"I want a photograph of us in the sea, and as much as I adore our guests, I wanted to tell you how beautiful you look and how much I love you." He kissed me tenderly on the mouth.

My stomach flipped and I laid my head in the crook of his neck, feeling the love flow through us.

"Remind me how you feel about children again," I said as I smiled and looked him in the eye.

"The more the better, I've told you," he said as he kissed my cheek. I could hear cameras clicking away and I didn't care. I was completely in the moment. "So if I told you that I did a pregnancy test this morning and I think I could be about six weeks pregnant, you wouldn't be upset?"

He stopped, mouth open eyes smiling before breaking into a huge grin. "Are you kidding me? I couldn't have asked for a better wedding present," he said as he spun me around.

"Fill your glasses, guys" Gregg shouted as he walked out of the sea. "I have just received the best wedding present ever." He waited, for effect. "We are going to be parents in approximately eight months' time!" he yelled.

Lots of noise followed with hugs, tears and kisses all round. It was the perfect day and I had never felt happier.

Seven months and five days after our wedding, Emily Rose was born, weighing in at four kilos. Nicki and Gregg were my birthing partners and Brent stayed in the background to support them both, and yes, I got my wish because Nicki and Brent were now a couple.

Emily had a shock of dark hair like Gregg, and Gregg had said that she looked like an English rose with her porcelain skin, hence the middle name.

I looked at my daughter as she lay sleeping in her bassinet and I thanked God for giving me the strength to move forward with my life and I realised that life really was full of miracles. You just have to hang on in there until one comes your way.